Undead and Unwelcome

"Packs a chic coffin." —*The Denver Post*

"Twists and turns to keep the readers hooked and longing for the next part." —*ParaNormalRomance*

"It will make you smile." —*The Best Reviews*

"A memorable visit with the Wyndham werewolves that fans should enjoy." —*Darque Reviews*

"Outrageously wacky." —*Romantic Times*

Undead and Uneasy

"A winner. Like sitting down to a cup of O-negative with a friend, catching up with the goings-on in Betsy's life is a real treat. Told with the irreverent humor Ms. Davidson's fans have come to expect." —*Fresh Fiction*

"Fans of Davidson's reluctant vampire queen will be thrilled . . . breezy dialogue, kick-ass action, and endearing characters." —*Booklist*

"A charming read whose creator never fails to make me smile . . . MaryJanice Davidson has the terrific ability to create characters that appeal, entertain, and endear themselves to readers." —*A Romance Review*

"Davidson—and her full-throated humor—is in top form. When it comes to outlandish humor, Davidson reigns supreme!" —*Romantic Times*

continued . . .

"Plenty of laugh-out-loud moments . . . I can't wait for the next installment of Undead." —*A Romance Review*

"Betsy is in fine form . . . Each story is better than the one before, and this one is no exception. Hurry, Ms. Davidson, I'm already ready for the next one. A very good read." —*Fresh Fiction*

Undead and Unappreciated

"The best vampire chick lit of the year . . . Davidson's prose zings from wisecrack to wisecrack." —*Detroit Free Press*

"A lighthearted vampire pastiche . . . a treat." —*Omaha World-Herald*

Undead and Unemployed

"One of the funniest, most satisfying series to come along lately. If you're fans of Sookie Stackhouse and Anita Blake, don't miss Betsy Taylor. She rocks." —*The Best Reviews*

"I don't care what mood you are in, if you open this book you are practically guaranteed to laugh . . . top-notch humor and a fascinating perspective of the vampire world." —*ParaNormalRomance*

Undead and Unwed

"Delightful, wicked fun!" —#1 *New York Times* bestselling author Christine Feehan

"Chick lit meets vampire action in this creative, sophisticated, sexy, and wonderfully witty book." —Catherine Spangler

"Hilarious." —*The Best Reviews*

Undead and Unwelcome

MaryJanice Davidson

JOVE BOOKS, NEW YORK

THE BERKLEY PUBLISHING GROUP
Published by the Penguin Group
Penguin Group (USA) Inc.
375 Hudson Street, New York, New York 10014, USA
Penguin Group (Canada), 90 Eglinton Avenue East, Suite 700, Toronto, Ontario M4P 2Y3, Canada
(a division of Pearson Penguin Canada Inc.)
Penguin Books Ltd., 80 Strand, London WC2R 0RL, England
Penguin Group Ireland, 25 St. Stephen's Green, Dublin 2, Ireland (a division of Penguin Books Ltd.)
Penguin Group (Australia), 250 Camberwell Road, Camberwell, Victoria 3124, Australia
(a division of Pearson Australia Group Pty. Ltd.)
Penguin Books India Pvt. Ltd., 11 Community Centre, Panchsheel Park, New Delhi—110 017, India
Penguin Group (NZ), 67 Apollo Drive, Rosedale, North Shore 0632, New Zealand
(a division of Pearson New Zealand Ltd.)
Penguin Books (South Africa) (Pty.) Ltd., 24 Sturdee Avenue, Rosebank, Johannesburg 2196,
South Africa

Penguin Books Ltd., Registered Offices: 80 Strand, London WC2R 0RL, England

This is a work of fiction. Names, characters, places, and incidents either are the product of the author's
imagination or are used fictitiously, and any resemblance to actual persons, living or dead, business
establishments, events, or locales is entirely coincidental. The publisher does not have any control
over and does not assume any responsibility for author or third-party websites or their content.

UNDEAD AND UNWELCOME

A Jove Book / published by arrangement with the author

PRINTING HISTORY
Berkley Sensation hardcover edition / June 2009
Jove mass-market edition / May 2010

Copyright © 2009 by MaryJanice Alongi.
Excerpt from *Undead and Unfinished* by MaryJanice Davidson copyright © by MaryJanice Alongi.
Cover art by Don Sipley.
Cover design by Lesley Worrell.
Text design by Kristin del Rosario.

ISBN: 978-0-515-14792-6

JOVE®
Jove Books are published by The Berkley Publishing Group,
a division of Penguin Group (USA) Inc.,
375 Hudson Street, New York, New York 10014.
JOVE® is a registered trademark of Penguin Group (USA) Inc.
The "J" design is a trademark of Penguin Group (USA) Inc.

PRINTED IN THE UNITED STATES OF AMERICA

10 9 8 7 6 5 4 3 2 1

Acknowledgments

For my mother-in-law, Elinor Alongi, who will slow down on her own terms, thank you. And, as for the rest of you idiots, after *you've* squeezed out four babies and raised them practically on your own and then buried your husband, if you want to pick the Thanksgiving menu, then by God, you're gonna pick it!

And for my sister-in-law, Julie Kathryn Gottlieb, who will run her house as she pleases, who struggled mightily to bring her dear son, Sam, into this world, who works for a multinational corporation while shopping, cooking, cleaning, and worrying about her widowed mother, and who, if she wants to change the Thanksgiving menu at the last minute, then by God, she's gonna change it!

I try to imagine my life with dull in-laws and I just—I just . . . I lock up. Tilt. Overload. Can't be done. Boring in-laws? What do they do? Just get along and be nice all the time? And never funny? N-never? *Never* funny? They just . . . I dunno . . . treat each other with a certain kind dignity and respect? *Respect?* Yeesh, I actually threw up in my mouth a little bit at the thought.

Boring relatives. Seems like a curse, don't it?

I am not cursed.

Two thousand eight was a mondo-busy year. And a difficult year in many ways—deaths in the family were the worst of it, and only the beginning. But the show must go on, and with the help of many people, the show did.

Given that I have the long-term memory of a salamander, I'm not going to try to name them all. There are too many, and I've mentioned many of them before and embarrassed the majority. To them, and everyone else, thank you, thank you, a thousand times thank you.

You've all helped me turn daydreams into fictional characters, helped me create whole worlds. These characters, to my surprise, have helped my readers get through difficult times. Which is something I never imagined my scribbling could ever do.

But readers have brought Betsy books to their chemo treatments. To counseling sessions. And, most horrifying of all, to family reunions.

That would be fine on its own, but they've also helped me use my work to help people who end up in jams . . . something that's happened to all of us at least once.

The bottom line? I've done nothing for you. Any of you. I write books because I get off on it; other people enjoying the work never entered my teeny, tiny mind. But you've sure helped me.

And that, I *won't* forget.

—MaryJanice Davidson
December 2008

Author's Note

I have never once spotted a werewolf on Cape Cod. But there are a lot of Wyndhams on Cape Cod. Draw your own conclusions.

Also, young werewolves really *aren't* at all like preadolescent humans. Don't let the cherubic faces fool you. It's a mistake you likely won't get to make twice.

Finally, Zyr vodka does exist, but not in the flavors Marc notes in his freezer. And thank goodness.

The Story So Far

Betsy ("Please don't call me Elizabeth") Taylor was run over by a Pontiac Aztec almost three years ago. She woke up as the Queen of the Vampires and in dazzling succession (in no particular order), she bit her friend Nick Berry; moved from a suburb to a mansion in St. Paul; solved various murders; lost her father and stepmother; became her half brother's guardian; continued to avoid the room housing the *Book of the Dead*; cured her best friend's cancer; visited her alcoholic grandfather (twice); solved a number of kidnappings; realized her husband, King Eric Sinclair, could read her thoughts (she could always read his); found out the Fiends had been up to no good (**Fiend:** [noun] a vampire given only [dead] animal blood; a vampire who quickly goes feral).

Also, Antonia, a werewolf from Cape Cod, took a bullet in the brain for Betsy, saving her life. The stories about bullets not hurting vampires are not true; plug enough lead into brain matter and that particular denizen of the undead will never get up again. Finally, Garrett, Antonia's lover, killed himself the instant he realized she was dead.

It's been a tough couple of years.

Unwelcome: ill-favored, inadmissible, objectionable, unacceptable, unwanted.

—ROGET'S II: THE NEW THESAURUS,
THIRD EDITION, 1995

Someone who is persona non grata is a foreigner officially **unwelcome** in another country. We use both terms in extended senses, mainly about people **unwelcome** or welcome in any figurative sense.

—THE COLUMBIA GUIDE TO
STANDARD AMERICAN ENGLISH

Undead and Unwelcome

Preview

He stared through the lens so hard he nearly gave himself a migraine. He looked away, then back, then away again.

The star remained. Hanging like a diamond against black velvet, it glowed and beckoned.

After some minutes of this, maybe an hour, he finally lunged for his cell phone and stabbed in a phone number he had memorized more than fifteen years ago.

It rang three times before a groggy voice answered, "Do you know what time it is?"

"I know exactly what time it is." He took a deep breath and pressed a hand against his chest. If he wasn't careful, he'd overexcite himself right into a coronary. "It's the time we've been praying for."

A short silence, followed by, "I'm getting up. I'll call the others."

"You do that." He hung up and went back to staring at the star. He couldn't look away. It called him.

Soon it would call them all.

Chapter 1

So, if I'm reading this correctly, you're a vampire now. Not a secretary."

"Not an administrative assistant," I corrected automatically. I mean, jeez! I knew Cooper was old and creaky, but what century did he think we were living in? (Or in my case, dying in and then reliving?)

"The important bit," Cooper went on, "is about the vampire."

"Well, yeah."

"And how you're the queen of them."

I sighed and flopped into an airplane seat. I examined the toes of my navy blue Cole Haan Penny Air

Loafers . . . not a scratch so far. "I guess some people would consider that an important point. The queen thing."

"It's bulleted and boldfaced. Also, the date of your death is in italics, along with how you don't have to urinate anymore."

"My pee or the lack thereof is nobody's business!" I gnashed my teeth and added, "Give me that."

I snatched the memo away from Cooper so quickly, he didn't see my hand move until his wrinkly fingers were clutching air. This startled him into a gasp, which we then both pretended I hadn't heard. That, I was learning, was vampire etiquette. Or, that is, vampire etiquette when dealing with humans. I'd finally figured it out after three years of being undead.

There should be a class, you know. Vampire Etiquette When Dealing with Humans 101. In another fifty years, I could teach the stupid thing.

I scanned the memo, my eyes bulging so much they felt like they were trying to leap from my skull. Cooper hadn't been kidding. Jessica *had* sent him a memo detailing my bodily functions. Two pages!

To: *Samuel Cooper.*
From: *The Boss.*
Re: *Betsy, Vampirism, and Cargo.*

Cargo? My gut churned.

And the part about me being the vampire queen *was* bulleted.

"I can't believe she sent you a memo."

"She always does. And I send 'em to her. Increasing fuel costs, licensing issues, route changes. You know how expensive fuel's getting now that China's buying all the oil? The E.M. ain't cheap, you know." The E.M.: Jessica's private joke. It stood for *Emancipated Minor.*

"And she sends her memos to me to keep me in the loop, don't you know. Seems this one's a little late, though," he muttered.

" 'Creepy speed and unnaturally grotesque super-strength'?" Aghast, I kept reading as other blechy phrases leaped out at me. " 'Still obsessed with shoes but married rich and can now actually afford the stupid things'? That scrawny traitor, I'm going to—agh! 'Immortality hasn't given her any interest in any topic she cannot refer to in the first person.'

Why, that—okay, I can't really argue with that last one, but she didn't have to highlight it. Look! It's *highlighted*."

"So is 'extreme narcissistic tendencies.' In any case, I'm to fly you to Cape Cod, so you can meet with the King of the Werewolves and make sure he doesn't sic his pack on you."

"I think it's pronounced *Pack*."

Cooper heard the capital *P* and nodded. "Right. This Pack, they're pretty ticked? Because of that little gal Antonia?"

I nibbled on the inside of my lip, distressed, as always, by any mention of Antonia. It had only been a week. It didn't still sting, as much as feel like a lateral slice through the liver.

See, poor Antonia was making the trip with us—in the cargo hold, as all corpses flew. In a plain wooden coffin, the lethal bullet holes all over her skull still not filled in by an undertaker. My husband, Sinclair, and I had no idea what werewolf funeral customs entailed, so we'd given orders that her body simply be placed in a coffin and loaded onto Jessica's private plane.

We didn't even wash her beautiful, dear face.

6

But that was nothing compared to what we did with Garrett's body.

"Look, Cooper, the important thing is now you know what you're getting into. So if you can't fly us out there, or if you think you—"

"Bite your tongue, miss. Or missus, I suppose. I've been flying for Jessica Wilson since she was seven years old, don't you know, and we've had hairy days and we've had *hairy days*."

"Cooper, I never, ever want to hear about your hair."

He ignored me. It was just as well. "I've seen and heard things—never mind, that's private family business."

"Oh, come on, we're best friends. I mean, Jessica and me." I didn't know if Cooper *had* any friends. "There's no way you know stuff that I don't—"

Cooper ruthlessly interrupted my shameless scrounging for gossip. "*This* doesn't scare me." He nodded at the memo, inadvertently crumpled in my fist. "But I surely wish Miss Jessica had told me earlier."

He meant, of course, "Like, how about before I flew you and the vampire king to New York City for your honeymoon, dumbass?" But Cooper neither a) freaked out, nor b) quit. And thank God, because finding another private pilot at this hour would have been a bitch.

"You got a problem with the boss?" I asked. "Take it up with the boss. What I want to know is, are we still leaving at eight o'clock?" Because if we weren't, I (and probably my husband) was going to be in big trouble with seventy-five thousand were-wolves. I held my breath, remembered for the thousandth time I didn't have to breathe anyway, and waited for his answer.

Chapter 2

Memos don't slow down my flight check," Cooper semiscolded in his luscious Irish accent. I managed not to swoon with relief. Also, oooh, European accents, I could listen to them all day. Americans sounded like illiterate bumpkins by comparison. "*Gunshots* don't slow down my flight check."

"Don't worry. Nobody's packing." On this flight.

"I could tell you stories about the carnage and body counts . . ." Cooper's pale blue eyes went misty with nostalgia while I watched him nervously, then he seemed to shake himself. "But the government made me promise."

"Well, hoo-ray for the government."

Cooper had first worked for Jessica's dad and, when her folks died (an ugly yet fitting death and a story for another time) and their assets transferred to her, he kept right on flying for her.

And as he'd said, Cooper heard things. Chances were he'd already known I was walking around dead. He was just miffed that Jessica hadn't told him three years ago.

And you know, he wasn't revolting looking. Tall—my height—with eyes the color of new denim and a shock of pure white hair that he wore over his shoulders, he was like an ancient hippy, albeit one who had never touched drugs nor alcohol.

He was wearing what Jessica teasingly called his uniform: khaki shorts, sandals, and a T-shirt that read, JESUS SAVES. HE PASSES TO NOAH. NOAH SCORES! He had tons of weird Jesus shirts. People picked fights if he wore the wrong T-shirt to the wrong place. Fights Cooper always won, despite his age. It was unreal, yet cool . . . sort of like Cooper himself. Jessica had fired him dozens of times for his own safety, but he always showed up the next day.

"Okay, then." I stood, forgetting I had been sitting under a bulkhead, and banged my head. "Ow!"

"Luckily being dead hasn't dulled your natural grace."

"Shut up, Cooper."

He smirked and tipped two fingers in a mock salute.

"All right, so I'll see you in another hour or so. They're, um, they're done loading Antonia and my husband's pulling together some paperwork . . ."

For what, I had no idea—Sinclair had his fingers in a lot of pies, and I wasn't interested enough to ask. He might answer, and then I'd have to listen. Or look like I was listening, which was harder than it sounded.

"Anyway," I finished, having almost lost my train of thought (again), "we'll be back a little later."

"I'll be ready, mum."

Oh, it was *mum* now? What was I, the queen of—never mind. "And for the zillionth time: Betsy. It's Betsy."

"Whatever you say, mum."

Polite as always, he didn't turn his back on me while I scuttled out of the plane and down the stairs. My car was parked on the west end of the tarmac of the Minneapolis airport; I had no idea what strings

Sinclair had pulled so that I could park there. I didn't want to know, frankly.

Okay, "my car" was a bit of an exaggeration . . . I'd driven one of Sinclair's to the airport for my little hey-guess-what-I'm-dead meeting. It was a Lexus hybrid, the only SUV I could drive without feeling like another planet-polluting asshole. Also, it had seat warmers.

There! One unpleasant chore out of the way—Cooper knew the scoop and, even better, hadn't tried to jam a cross down my throat. He'd agreed to fly us to the Cape, and best of all, hadn't tried to offer me a washcloth soaked in holy water. Another sneezing fit I so did not need.

Have I mentioned there are some actual perks to being the long-prophesied vampire queen? I'm so used to bitching about my unwanted crown I tend to overlook the positives.

Holy water, crosses, and stakes can't hurt me. Nor garlic. Antonia, my dear dead friend, had no idea if bullets would kill me, and refused to risk my life to find out. Which is why she was riding in the cargo hold instead of the plush seats of a private plane.

I shoved Antonia out of my head; it still hurt too much to think about her sacrifice.

And speaking of sacrifices, there was Garrett, Antonia's late lover, to think about. Once he'd realized that Antonia was dead—in part due to his own cowardice—he'd killed himself right in front of us. Messily.

I didn't quite dare broach the subject with Sinclair; he felt unrivaled contempt for a lover who would jam someone up and then not face the consequences.

Me, I wasn't so sure it was that black and white. Garrett was never strong. He was never even brave. But he had loved Antonia and couldn't live without her. Literally.

Tina and Sinclair had taken care of his body, dragging it off the broken staircase (poor Garrett looked like he'd been caught in a giant set of teeth), cutting off the head, and burying it at Nostro's old farm (where the Fiends . . . the ones still alive . . . lived).

But that was enough of that for now—Garrett was dead, and I couldn't change that. But I was going to have a word with my alleged best friend about her irritating, insulting, and idiotic memorandum (memoranda?).

I mean, jeez. Narcissistic? Didn't she stop to think how *I* would feel if Cooper read that about me? Not to mention, I wasn't even cc'd on the thing.

I swear, I didn't know what had gotten into that girl since I'd cured her cancer and she had to dump her boyfriend because he hated my guts. Frankly, I've been having a terrible time this week.

And now rogue memos! It was too much for anyone to expect me to handle, which I would be pointing out to her the minute I saw her.

Self-centered? Me? Sometimes that girl doesn't know me at all.

Chapter 3

Dear Myself Dude,

I can't remember the last time I tried to write in a diary. This one will go the way the others went, I think. I'll write like gangbusters for a week or two, then lose all interest in writing about my life and get back to living my life. But here I am again, starting a diary for the first time in over twenty years.

That's a lie, of course. One of my psych profs told me in college that we lie best when we lie to ourselves.

The man knew his shit. I know exactly when I quit writing in diaries: it was right around the time I realized I had zero interest in girls, but plenty of interest in boys. I was fourteen, and kept waiting to grow out of it. Kept wondering what was wrong with me. Hoped it was just a phase. Prayed my father wouldn't find out. Prayed no one in high school would find out.

The trouble with being a closeted homosexual is exactly this: you live with the agonizing fear you will be found out.

I hid until I was old enough to drink.

When I was sixteen, I tore up my last diary for the simplest and most cowardly of reasons: I didn't want my dad to find it. Colonel Phillip P. Spangler's only son a bum puncher? A faggot? A crank gobbler? He would have killed me, or I would have killed me, so best to stop writing things like "I wish Steve Dillon would dump that idiot cheerleader and blow me for an hour or two."

So. Diaries. Specifically, new diaries. No chance the colonel will find this one; he's in hospice, crankily dying of lung cancer.

It's pretty rotten that I wasn't sad when I heard. It's worse that I reran his labs myself to confirm it. I was relieved. Poor excuse for a man's only son.

My name is Marc Spangler. I'm a doctor, an ER resident at one of the busier Minneapolis hospitals, and I live in a mansion. No, I am not rich. Not yet . . . and probably not ever, unless I specialize in cardiology, oncology, or face-lifts. Fortunately, this is not the sort of job you go into in order to make money. Which is a good thing, because I found out (quite by accident) that when you break down my shifts into hourly rates, every receptionist in the building makes more money than I do.

But back to the mansion. My best friends are a vampire and the richest woman in the state of Minnesota (and, as Jessica herself would point out, not the richest black woman . . . the richest woman). In fact, they are my only friends. Once I left the shithole I grew up in, I never went back. And I never will.

I haven't gotten laid in a while, but on the upside, I lead the most interesting life of anyone I know . . . except maybe for Betsy and Sinclair, the King and Queen of the Vampires.

Ooooh, Sinclair. Don't get me started. Tall, broad-shouldered, dark hair, dark eyes, long fingers, and when he and Betsy go at it, the entire mansion shakes. Those are usually the nights I go out and get drunk.

Mostly because I've always been wildly attracted

to him, and partly because Betsy has unconsciously worked her charm on me . . . she's about the only woman I've ever seriously considered sleeping with. And—don't get me wrong, dude, because I love her to death—it's just as well we didn't hook up. What with the shoe shopping and the bitching about being stuck in a job she didn't ask for and didn't want, and the way she manages (quite unconsciously, I'm sure) to make everything about her . . . nope, nope, nope. If she was my girlfriend, I probably would have jammed a needle full of potassium into my heart before the end of the first week.

She has twenty-eight pairs of black pumps. Twenty-eight! I counted them myself. Then I counted again to make sure I wasn't hallucinating, and got twenty-nine. Those twenty-eight or -nine pairs were maybe a third of her collection. Her love for fine footgear . . . it's almost pathological.

Thing is, while I was debating trying sex from the other side of the fence, Betsy didn't even know she was doing it. Getting into my head, inspiring me to wear a bit more aftershave than I usually do, making me want her . . . she did it completely unknowingly and by accident. My inner scientist wished I could have known her in life, so I could compare her premortem charisma with her "vampire mojo," as she called it.

And why am I going on and on about Betsy's unholy sex appeal? That's not what I wanted to say at all.

Basically, I guess I've started another diary because things aren't all happy-happy-yay-yay, the-good-guys-win anymore. I thought I'd learned that by the time I was in my fourth year of medical school, but I didn't know shit about death back then.

I know a lot more, now.

People are dying. Good guys are dying. Friends are dying. And I just figure someone ought to be writing it all down.

Because one of these days, I'm worried they'll be flying me in a private plane and I won't be riding in first class, if you know what I mean.

The colonel might care. Might. I won't be around to see it, so I guess it doesn't matter.

Chapter 4

My husband grimaced as I plopped down next to him with BabyJon in my arms. Not particularly keen on fatherhood in the first place, Eric had found it an annoying shock that his wife was the legal guardian of her infant half brother.

He was, like any man, jealous of anything that took his wife's attention away from him (which was part cute and part irritating).

Also, it was my fault my father and stepmother were dead (long story short: cursed engagement ring, grants wishes, and the cost is always high). And when I used the ring, my father was killed. As well as my stepmother.

I had wished for a baby of my own and, like that

story "The Monkey's Paw," my wish was granted in a rather grisly way: With BabyJon's parents dead, guess who got custody? Bingo. Leaving me with an instant baby, zero stretch marks, and a ton of buried guilt.

Since I had inadvertently made BabyJon an orphan, I figured the *least* I could do was raise him. He was my only shot at motherhood; obviously, dead people don't breed.

He squirmed in my arms. I smiled at him. Jet-black hair and crystal blue eyes, plump where babies are supposed to be plump. (Enjoy society's acceptance of your body fat while it lasts, baby brother.) He had four teeth so far, and his lower lip was a waterfall of drool.

"Why not put him in his seat?" my husband asked, shaking out the *Wall Street Journal* like it was a beach blanket.

"Because we're not going anywhere right this second."

"Not yet!" Jessica called from the cockpit. She took off her headphones—she thought they made her look cool, when I knew she was listening to the latest Shakira album—and headed toward us.

She plopped into the seat behind us and curled up like a cat. She was so small, she actually pulled it off.

"So we're really doing this thing?"

Sinclair looked around as if verifying the cockpit, the pilot, his papers, my magazines. "It appears so."

"Because, for the record? I think it's nuts. What happened to that poor girl wasn't your fault."

"Sure," I said, shocked at how bitter I sounded. It felt like I was sucking on a psychic lemon. "I'll blame the next-door neighbor's dog."

"Not Muggles?" Jessica gasped, which made me snicker in spite of myself. She could always do that. I was awfully glad she hadn't died.

"Even if Elizabeth felt no sense of responsibility, bringing the body back is respectful."

And it lets you get a good look at the maybe-bad guys, doesn't it, hot stuff? But I kept that stuff to myself; it was pillow talk, and none of Jessica's business.

She probably knew, though. Sinclair would no more let an advantage like that slip (meeting a powerful force in neutral territory) than he would go outside without pants.

"But I would like to add once again—"

"Oh, here we go."

"I don't think you should accompany us, Jessica. It's likely to be dangerous."

Jessica waved her sticklike arms around. She

could put an eye out with one of those things. "Since Betsy came back from the dead, what isn't? Shit. I can't even go to the Mall of America without running into a sniper team."

"You exaggerate."

"Yes, but not by much."

Sinclair shrugged. "As you like." He knew, as we all did, that it was Jessica's plane. And that she'd insist on coming even if it was *his* plane.

In some ways, and I know this sounds terrible, but in some ways it was almost bad that I'd cured her cancer. Now she was in the middle of this whole "lust for life" thing and was being more of a tagalong than usual.

I'd cured her by accident, which was terrific. But I'd also made her fearless by accident, which wasn't. There'd come a day—the law of averages demanded it—when I wouldn't be around to save her teeny butt.

"You know, Sinclair's got a point," I began, knowing I was wasting my time (I had no actual breath to waste). "Who knows what the reception's going to be like? There's still time to get off this crazy train and—"

"Taking off right about now, ma'am," Cooper called.

"You did that on purpose," I muttered.

Up front, Cooper was doing his flight check while

Jessica climbed out of her seat, walked to the front (the fore? The cabin? I was many things, but a pilot wasn't one of them), and took her seat next to Cooper.

She couldn't fly and only had a passing knowledge of the instruments Cooper used, but it *was* her plane. I figured someday she would summon the nerve to ask him to teach her.

Jessica's presence was less problematic for Cooper than for me, which is a horrible thing to say about a best friend. As I said, I'd cured her of a lethal blood disease, totally by accident.

But while the vampire in me had once cured her cancer, it had also attacked her. It had also ripped her boyfriend from her and leeched off her generous spirit.

Every time I looked at her I worried, and resolved to deserve her, and then worried again.

To distract myself I stood up, popped BabyJon into his car seat, made sure it was secured to the airplane seat, and then sat back down to buckle my own seat belt. Little brother stared out the window without making so much as a peep.

Wait. Buckle my seat belt? Should I bother? Could a plane crash even hurt me? I looked down at Eric's waistline and saw that he hadn't bothered.

Huh. Well. Old habits, you know?

24

"Aren't you nervous?" I asked.

"Extremely."

"I'm being serious."

"Oh." The newspaper slowly came down. "My pardon, dear one. Nervous about what? Facing down an unknown number of opponents as strong and fast as we are? Or surviving a plane flown by an Irishman?"

"Nasty! What'd the Irish ever do to you?"

"Never mind," he muttered darkly. "It was a long time ago."

"Just focus on not dying, and we'll be fine."

He smiled and cupped my chin in his hand. In a second, our faces were only inches apart. "I shall promise not to die, but only if you do so as well."

"Deal," I murmured, having no idea what I was agreeing to. Being this close to Sinclair often had this effect on me.

"Taking off now, ladies and gents," Cooper said, the party pooper.

Sinclair took his hand away and picked up the paper; I just stared at the ceiling. That was how we began the long taxi toward a place I had never been and didn't particularly want to go.

With a corpse somewhere under my feet. Mustn't forget that.

Chapter 5

A few hours later, we were descending the stairs (except for Cooper, who stayed behind to do whatever it is pilots do after passengers exit) to the Logan Airport tarmac.

I winced when I saw Antonia's coffin brought out and carefully laid down.

For such a huge airport, I was surprised at how quiet Logan was . . . it seemed almost deserted. I figured that was because we were at the part where they parked the private planes.

Three people were waiting for us on the tarmac, clustered around a vehicle that was a cross between a limo and a hearse.

I recognized them right away. Michael Wynd-ham, Pack leader (and, though this wasn't the time or place, so so cute, with golden brown hair and calm yellow eyes). His wife, Jeannie, a blonde with a head full of fluffy curls (must be hell in the humidity). And Derik, one of Michael's werewolves, also yummilicious with short-cropped yellow blond hair and green eyes. Was being gorgeous written into the werewolf genetic code?

Well, wait. Jeannie was human, though the others weren't. We'd met the week I got married (long, *long* story) and I'd gotten a bit of her history then. I guess, for Michael and Jeannie, it had been love at first sight.

As opposed to the loathe at first sight it had been for Sinclair and me. Ah, memories.

If nothing else, I hoped that my prior meeting with Jeannie might help smooth things over. The woman had helped me pick out my wedding gown, for heaven's sake. There was a *bond* there, dammit.

I'd met Derik and Michael that same week, and though Michael gave off "cool leader" vibes, Derik was a ball of good-humored energy.

Usually.

We faced each other through a long, uncomfortable silence. Finally, I cleared my throat to say something when Derik walked over to the coffin and started to—

Oh, man. He wasn't. He wasn't. He . . . was. He was lifting the lid off.

"I don't think that's a good idea," my husband said quietly, and I seized his hand and squeezed, which would have pulverized the bones in an ordinary human's hand, but would have as much effect on Sinclair as a mosquito bite.

He squeezed back, which hurt.

"Derik, Eric's right," Michael warned. Under the fluorescent lights, he was as pale as milk. They all were, actually. Poor, poor guys. I wasn't sure who I pitied more: the dead Antonia or the living Pack members.

"I need to be sure," Derik insisted, and I winced again. The poor guy had pinned all his hopes on the chance that we'd gotten another werewolf mixed up with Antonia, which was so dumb I wanted to cry.

The lid was all the way up. Derik stared inside for a long moment and then, with infinite care, slowly lowered the lid.

Then he started to howl.

Chapter 6

We were all shocked, even his friends were shocked. Derik, normally a man of sunny temperament (at least from what I'd seen a few months back), was roaring like a rabid bear. Then he raised his fists over his head and brought them crashing down on the coffin lid, which instantly gave way.

Suddenly it was hard for me to swallow. Suddenly I wanted a drink in the worst way. Any drink. A smoothie, a frozen mudslide, blood, gasoline, Clorox, whatever.

Derik was glaring at me with eyes that were hard to look away from. "You might have washed her face, at least."

This was my evening for wincing, except this time it was almost a flinch. Because Derik was right . . . but then, was I wrong in trying to show respect for whatever rituals they had?

Jessica coughed and spoke up, attempting to save my ass. "We, um, didn't want to offend you guys."

"Offend?" Derik spat. And in a flash, I remembered Antonia once telling me that her only real friend in the Pack was Derik. *"Offend?"*

Crash! More fist-sized holes in the lid, which he seemed determined to convert into thousands of velvet-tipped toothpicks. I took a step forward . . . only to feel Sinclair's hand close around my bicep and gently pull me back.

He was right, of course. This wasn't about me, and stomping into the middle of it would have been grossly inappropriate. And yet. And still. I couldn't stand seeing anyone—even a bare acquaintance—in so much pain.

My feet seemed determined to disobey my brain, because they took another slow step . . . and Sinclair tugged me back, not so gently this time.

"You never should have gone!" Derik was yelling into the coffin. "You stupid bitch! You left your Pack!"

Nobody said anything to that, big surprise. Because, again, it was the truth.

"All right, that's enough," Michael said calmly. His copper-colored eyes looked almost orange in the fluorescents. "Let's take her home, Derik."

So into the back Antonia went, the way back where there were no seat belts, because none were needed.

Jeannie drove; Michael sat beside her in the front. Derik sat across from us in the back. Looking through us, not at us.

No one said a word during the entire ninety-minute drive to Cape Cod.

Chapter 7

esus!" I gasped, staring out the window. Sinclair flinched, but I was used to his twitches. "*This* is where you live?" I asked, feeling like I had straw in my hair and cow shit on my heels. All I needed were a few "hyuk, hyuks!" to complete the picture. "You *live* here?"

"Yes," Michael said shortly as he drove to the main entrance. I pressed my face up against the window so hard my nose squashed. Thanks to no longer being addicted to oxygen, I didn't fog up the glass, at least.

It was a castle.

No, really. A castle. On Cape Cod! And I wasn't the only impressed yokel: both Jessica (who'd napped all the way here, like BabyJon) and Sinclair (who'd grown up on a farm a zillion years ago) were staring out their windows, too.

Gravel crunched beneath the wheels as we neared the castle of red bricks and red stones with about a zillion windows, set square in the middle of a huge field of green, with the Atlantic Ocean right behind it and stretching all the way into a gray forever. If it looked this magical at night, how, oh how, would it look during the day?

I promised myself I would find out. If you're going to get stuck with an eternal membership card of the undead, being the prophesied queen was the way to go. Not only did I wake up in the afternoon, instead of sunset, but I could go outside. I'd never burn up, not to mention worry about wrinkles and freckles. It was like getting your hand stamped at a club, only a zillion times cooler.

I realized I was still sitting in the car like a startled blond lump, and yanked on the door handle. I could hear the murmur of waves as I got out of the limo. Could smell the salt in the air, the sweetness of the grass field. Tilted my head back and looked at a sky of stars I had never seen before, dangling over the pure ocean.

I almost went into sensory overload, to be honest; it was a gorgeous night and, by God, it *smelled* gorgeous and I was absolutely loving my enhanced senses (which had not always been the case, believe me— don't even get me started on Marc's aftershave).

Until I got here, I hadn't known that gorgeous could *be* a smell.

"It's late," Michael said curtly, striding up to the main doors with Jeannie almost in lockstep beside him. Sinclair was also abreast of them. (How did he *do* that, just fall into step right beside the biggest and strongest like he belonged there?)

So I tried to stop gaping and trotted after Jessica, who was trotting herself to keep up. I'd unhooked BabyJon's car seat and carried it with us, though it suddenly felt like it was full of several gold bars as I hurried and sniffed and looked around and kept my grip hard enough so that the seat didn't bang against my shins. Good Lord, I was really getting out of shape if a simple walk to a house . . . *castle* . . . taxed my attention, not to mention my balance.

"And we have a lot to talk about."

Eh? Oh, right. Michael was talking. I should absolutely be listening.

"Gee, ya think?" Jessica whispered to me. "And here I thought we were here for the lobster."

I smothered a laugh, knowing that even if Antonia and Garrett weren't dead this was no time to get the giggles. We had a pretty scary itinerary and never mind the seafood jokes (though I wondered if I could eat clam chowder). Maybe it seemed weird for a vampire to fret or be stressed—this vampire, at least—but despite how it always looks in books and movies, whole weeks—*months*—could pass by without any life-or-death bullshit.

Not last week, though. I thought the early part of the week had bitten the big one, what with the Fiends going all, you know, fiendish, solving the murders, avoiding my own murder (something I was starting to get good at just from sheer repetition, and wasn't *that* the opposite of amusing), and being a helpless witness to a murder/suicide in my foyer. Okay, technically Jessica's foyer.

So Antonia was dead, Garrett had killed himself, but the fun wasn't over yet, which is why I was standing in front of the Atlantic Ocean instead of the Mississippi River.

Yeah, I figured we'd all earned about six years

off—shoot, I was still a newlywed, I had a pile of thank-you notes yet to write—but the joke was on me, as it so often is, and all the tears and terror and bullets meant for me had only brought us to Wednesday. Now it was the weekend, and Sinclair and I had a fresh set of problems.

First and foremost, how big a mess *was* this? How much blame would fall on my friends and me, how much did we deserve . . . or need to dodge? Most important, what were the werewolves cloistered here going to do about it? About us? And how could I explain Antonia's former-Fiend boyfriend to werewolves, without going too far and screwing over my own people?

Had Antonia ever even told her Pack she'd been sleeping with a vampire? I should have known the answer to that. But Antonia had always made it clear that her phone calls with Michael were Pack business, and we all tried to respect her privacy.

Only to the werewolves, it would probably look like negligence, or carelessness.

I had never wanted a drink so badly in my life.

We followed Michael up redbrick stairs and into a vestibule the size of a ballroom. I stared . . .

Sure, why not? You've been gaping like a tourist

*instead of an invited head of state. Which is just
fine, because you'll never fool a real leader.*

`. . .` while trying not to look like I was doing so.
This place made our mansion on Summit Avenue—
one of the prettiest, grandest, richest streets in the
Midwest—look like a one-bedroom apartment in
the warehouse district. Michael's castle . . .

*Yep, now there's a real leader, so quit fakin',
bacon.*

`. . .` was lit up in a blaze of lights (mostly from
the overhead chandeliers) and what little furniture I
could see was mahogany. The place smelled like old
wood and cedar, floor wax and furniture. It was the
most impressive dwelling I'd ever seen, and I'd only
seen a tenth of a fraction of it.

We climbed a grandly sweeping flight of stairs
(Marble floors! Marble floors! Werewolves must not
ever slip, or maybe they just hated vacuuming), followed the Wyndhams down a wide hallway carpeted
in red (not the red you might think, an orangey red,
a dark pink—no, this was *red* red, a deep, rich, true
red), and were soon in a room twice as big as my
kitchen that was clearly Michael's office.

He probably filled out paperwork, or clipped cou-
pons, or downloaded songs from iTunes when he

wasn't ruling the world from behind the ginormous desk almost directly across from us. And excuse me, had I described the grand piano–sized, reddish brown, beautifully appointed, gleaming chunk of wood as a desk?

More fool me. The President of the U.S. sat behind a desk. Elementary school teachers sat behind desks. Prison wardens. Librarians. DMV employees. Desk sergeants. (Thus the name!) Reporters. Loan officers.

Those were desks. This thing was a wooden monument to Michael's status.

There were a few comfortable chairs scattered about, all dark wood with plush seats. Floor-to-ceiling bookshelves lined two of the walls; the other walls had windows and pictures and such. One framed portrait caught my eye—obviously old, but the people were familiar to me somehow, which was impossible.

I stepped closer and stared harder. No, I didn't know them. The man had lush dark hair and the woman had brown eyes—no, not brown, more golden than brown, more like—

More like Michael's.

Of course! The mater and pater of the Pack. Damn. Bet they'd known some good stories.

(*Can you hear them, Elizabeth?*)

I stifled a yelp of surprise and darted a look in Sinclair's direction. It was handy to be able to read your husband's mind, but that didn't mean I thought it was natural, normal, or not nerve-wracking. The fact that our telepathy tended to show only during extreme stress or excitement (making love, being murdered, trying to figure out if vampires have to pay property tax) told me something about Sinclair's state of mind.

My tall, dark darling might come across as calm and reasonable, even a little bored, and yet he was worried enough (about me? the whole group? both?) to pop his question right into my head, where I heard it as easily as if he was using a megaphone.

(*Elizabeth. Can you hear them?*)

Oh, right, you're probably expecting an answer. I nodded. Sure I could. And I knew what Sinclair was getting at. There wasn't a soul to be seen, and the castle seemed almost deserted, but it wasn't. Not even close to deserted. We could hear them walking around and, even worse, standing still. I was—don't ask me how—sure they were listening to us. Believe me, I know how it sounds: We could hear them listening to us? Give me a break.

Except we absolutely could. And that was the scariest thing of all, knowing the castle was full of monsters who really would eat you, just like an ogre in a fairy tale.

My, Grandma, what big ears you have.

My worry for Jessica increased by a factor of about eight hundred . . . she had nothing in the way of enhanced paranormal senses, but that didn't mean she wasn't picking up on the tension. Boy oh boy, I hoped we'd be able to make friends with the ogres. Which is a sentence I never thought I'd have to think, much less articulate.

Chapter 8

Drinks?" Jeannie asked, playing bartender. I was eyeing her hair with not a little admiration. Unlike mine, which at best could be coaxed to be wavy (I'd had a highlight touch-up and deep-conditioning treatment the week before I'd died; I might be a slavering ghoul of the undead, but I would never have graying split ends), hers was shoulder length, surfer blond, and curly . . . the kind that frizzed out in July, the kind that was a mass of soft spiral curls tonight. The rest of her was unexceptional.

Okay, that came out wrong . . . Jeannie Wyndham was a beautiful woman, admirably slim after two kids, casually dressed in jeans, loafers (Payless; ah, well, nobody's perfect), a soft blue chambray shirt, and a tan wool blazer.

When I described her as unexceptional, I meant in comparison to my surroundings: Michael's wife was the queen of everything I was staring at; it was all half hers. But you'd never know it to look at her; she had the brisk, understated demeanor of an experienced nurse.

Except for the eyes, of course; she had the flat and calculating gaze of a sniper. I wondered where her gun was. This was more than idle curiosity; the last time I'd seen her she'd shot me. Three times. In the chest.

But later she'd helped me pick out the greatest dress in the history of human garments, so I didn't hold it against her anymore. Attempted murder is a fleeting moment, but the perfect wedding gown lasts forever.

"Betsy? Drink?"

Damn, I was really gonna have to pay better attention. I'd been so busy staring around the room and remembering point-blank chest wounds that I took the glass without looking and drained it.

And nearly barfed all over the beautiful Persian rug. I *think* it was Persian. It looked expensive and smelled old. Michael's great-great-great-great-grandparents had probably hauled it all the way to Plymouth from the *Mayflower*, centuries after their great-great-great-great-grandparents had hauled it from the palace of Cyrus.

How did I know Cyrus was one of the first rulers of the Persians, you ask? Hey. I don't *always* ignore my husband when he's prattling on about useless stuff.

"*Wwwrrllgg!*" I managed, wiping off what was dribbling down my disgusted chin. I forced what was left of the loathsome liquid down. "What the hell is this, kerosene?"

"We're out of kerosene," Derik said with no trace of a smile. This was far from the Derik I'd met before, who had been all smiles, charming and sexy and nice.

"I should have mentioned that my wife only likes drinks that come from a dirty blender," Sinclair said. He was sitting across from Michael, who was behind his desk. I was sitting next to him; Jessica was on my right. Jeannie, done with handing out glasses of regurgitate, was pacing back and forth behind us. Like I wasn't already nervous enough. "I take it you didn't enjoy your first whiskey, dear one?"

Yeah, about as much as a tax audit, jerkhead. Guess I wasn't as thirsty as I'd thought.

Sinclair nodded thoughtfully, his fist pressed under his nose to hide a smile. He hadn't been reading my mind as long as I'd been able to read his (it's a long story, and I come off kind of bad in it), so he was still in the wow-this-is-so-awesome stage, whereas I was at the fuck-you-I-have-no-privacy phase.

I fumbled frantically in my purse, found a tin of Altoids, and dumped half of them in my mouth. I crunched them up like they were Rice Krispies, relishing the way the mint overpowered the yuck-o booze. Zow! The potent little buggers were really clearing out my sinuses; my eyes were all but watering. Which would have been a good trick, since my eyes don't water.

"Let me begin by saying we appreciate you bringing Antonia home to us."

"Nnnn prbm," I crunched, trying not to cough. Dammit! Probably shouldn't have dumped such a big mouthful into my gaping piehole. Probably shouldn't have done a lot of things this week.

"It was no trouble, and the least we could do," Sinclair said, speaking as calmly and colorlessly as Michael while I crunched furiously. I wondered if

44

that was the royal "we." "It was an honor to escort her back home."

"My understanding is that she was shot several times in the head, protecting you," Michael said calmly. Calmly, but a muscle beside his eye twitched.

I tried not to stare, and failed. I gave serious thought to getting up and spitting my mashed Altoids into his spotless wastebasket, but just didn't dare. It seemed . . . what was the word Eric would use? *Undiplomatic.*

With a mighty effort, I swallowed the minty lump down, gagged briefly, and sneezed. Beside me, I could sense Sinclair rolling his eyes and either trying not to smirk, or thinking up an excuse for me. I'd deal with him later.

"Yes, that's right," I replied with startlingly fresh breath. I managed to stifle the second sneeze. "She saved me."

"Why?"

Huh. That didn't seem very nice. My tongue ran away before I could stop it: "Because she lost a bet?"

There was a loud hissing sound, like everyone had gasped at the same time. I looked at my lap and muttered, "Sorry. Too soon?"

"What could bullets have done to a vampire?" Michael continued, unmoved by my terrific breath and sarcastic observations. And that was the $50,000 question. Because it was only recently that vampires realized werewolves existed, and vice versa. Michael probably assumed our vampirism was straight out of a bad horror movie. And who could blame him? I hadn't thought lead bullets would hurt a werewolf.

"What would bullets in the brain do to anyone?" Sinclair replied quietly, totally screwing up my assumption. "There was no chance anyone could have regenerated."

Michael had tipped back in his chair and was staring at the ceiling. "Mmmm." Then he had all four legs of his chair on the floor and met all our gazes.

Well. Almost all. His gaze kept skittering over the sleeping BabyJon. He hadn't asked one question about the baby, made one comment, not even a careless, "Cute kid." And from what I'd heard, he was a devoted dad who loved ankle biters, nose miners, whatever.

But he wouldn't look at BabyJon. And that was very strange. So strange it was starting to make me nervous.

"I hope the baby isn't bothering you," I said, to which Michael had no reply. Now he was locking gazes with Derik. It was like he hadn't even heard me—which was bullshit, given what I knew about werewolf hearing.

Why ignore an infant? To what purpose? And why was it making me so nervous?

I was rocking BabyJon's seat with my toe as he slept, trying to get a handle on my feelings. Hey, it wasn't like I had to worry about bad breath at the moment. Quite the opposite, in fact. And sure, this was a stressful scene, but they had all seemed nice enough when I'd met them earlier.

After all, we could have gotten a much nastier reception. Much nastier. But nobody had so much as waved a crucifix in our direction. No one had attacked us yet, to be sure. So why was I practically shaking?

Sinclair was frowning at me, picking up my nervousness, but not the cause. All I could do was lift my left shoulder in a tiny shrug, the international "tell you later" gesture.

Besides, I had other things to focus on. Derik, for instance. He'd been so different when he'd come to the mansion looking for Antonia a couple months back. Friendly and charming and funny and sooo cute . . . though I usually didn't go for blonds.

In fact, the only time he'd gotten upset was when he followed me to BabyJon's nursery and—and—

I could almost hear the *click* as the reason behind my sudden nervousness clunked home: Derik kept giving BabyJon a wide berth, and Michael didn't even seem to *see* him. Which was impossible; you couldn't hide a twenty-pound infant surrounded by a pastel car seat, not when he was right out on the floor and smelling like formula and stale powder.

Now that I thought about it, Jeannie was the only one who had acknowledged BabyJon; she had stroked his feathery black hair once we had him buckled in the limo, and complimented me on his good looks. I wasn't sure if I could take the credit for those or not, so I'd just nodded.

But Derik . . . Derik had followed me to the nursery once, taken one look at the baby, and nearly broken his neck on the stairs while trying to achieve distance. There was so much other shit going on at the time, I'd completely forgotten about it until now.

I dared not forget again . . . something was wrong with this baby. Or with any werewolf who came in contact with him.

And I didn't like that. At all.

Now Derik *and* Jeannie were pacing behind us, which was just as nerve-wracking as it sounds. But whenever Derik got near BabyJon, he would veer off. And Michael, as I said, couldn't see him at all.

And *they weren't even aware of it.* Derik could have been avoiding a mud puddle for all the emotion he showed, and Michael, who could and did hold everyone's gaze in the way only an alpha werewolf could, wasn't looking at BabyJon.

All of a sudden, I had a brand-new problem dumped in my lap. Just what I needed. I'd have rather had a new pair of Prada pumps dumped on me.

Chapter 9

Why did I seize so quickly on the possibility that BabyJon was special? Well, consider our sister, Laura, who was back in Minnesota but still very much in my thoughts as I whispered superminty breath across the mahogany expanse that separated me from the alpha male of Antonia's werewolf Pack.

Laura, an impossibly beautiful, naïve, and sweet blonde, was raised by a minister and his wife, which partially explained why she was currently a tireless worker for charities, as well as a cheerful and frequent Goodwill volunteer.

Laura worked in soup kitchens and went to church

on Sundays. She stuck twenty-dollar bills into red Salvation Army buckets at Christmastime (and Laura was far from rich; her folks made less in one year than Sinclair made in a month). In February she had literally given the shirt (well, the coat) off her back to someone down on her luck.

Sickening? Okay. Yes. A little. But still, it all made perfect sense. How else could someone rebel against their parent? Laura fought back by being sweet and kind. Mostly sweet. Although she had a spectacular temper.

Also, her birth mother (not the minister's wife) was the devil. Yes. The devil. As in Satan. As in Lucifer. As in a woman who looked weirdly like Lena Olin, except with better footgear. Either Satanic influence or Lena Olin's terrific fashion sense had endowed Laura with supernatural abilities—of course! She was half angel, right? Lucifer's lineage hadn't changed when he/she was tossed out of heaven.

And I was beginning to suspect BabyJon had powers, too. Not that we could confirm this by asking Lena-Satan—after possessing the birth mother long enough to experience breast-feeding and stretch marks, she had fled for the easier comforts of hell.

The minister and his wife who adopted Laura had been the best thing to happen to her, and kept her diabolic lineage in check.

So, I wondered, who will keep my half brother in check if he inherits anything unusual? Me? It was the only thing that made sense in an increasingly complicated family history.

(I have a point. I promise.)

Okay, I can see how some of this—most of this— could be confusing. Shit, it's my *life* and even I get mixed up sometimes. So. The Cliffs Notes version: the devil possessed my stepmother, the Ant, because she wanted to try the whole giving birth and raising a kid thing. My stepmother, the late Antonia Taylor (I know, I know . . . *two* Antonias? Both dead? What were the odds on something like that?) was so unrelievedly nasty, no one had any idea she was possessed.

Think about that for a minute. My stepmother was so horrible and nasty on a daily basis that *no one noticed* when she was possessed by the devil for almost a year.

I know! It boggles my mind, too.

Anyway, the devil had hated labor and delivery, not to mention breast-feeding and stretch marks, and fled my stepmother's body to get the hell back to hell.

When my stepmother realized that someone else had been running her body for *almost a year* (remember: nobody even noticed!), she promptly gave the baby up for adoption.

And didn't tell my father about it. Hey, the couple that lies together (no pun intended) stays together. Or however that saying goes.

Only the Ant knew my dad had fathered Laura, which is why she and I didn't meet until two decades later. My late father, who I'd always thought of as a colorless coward, had fathered the Beloved of the Morningstar (in other words, the Antichrist) and a vampire queen.

God help us if it turned out I had another half brother lurking out in the world somewhere; maybe he was the reincarnation of Attila the Hun. Maybe I should have talked Dad into having some of his sperm frozen.

Yuck. Time to get off the subject of my father's sperm.

Anyway, back to BabyJon. Now I was wondering— maybe it was silly . . . vampire queen or no, this stuff really wasn't my field—maybe my stepmother's body had retained some leftover magic from her days of possession. And maybe that had had a profound effect on her late-in-life baby.

Shoot, the poor kid had been conceived purely out of spite. The Ant had not liked it at all when her spoiled bimbo stepdaughter returned from the dead, so Ant tried to pull her husband's attention back to his second family with the age-old trick: she'd gotten pregnant to jazz up her marriage.

Michael was still talking. Jeannie and Derik were still pacing. Sinclair's face was serene and composed, but he kept glancing at me and I knew *he* knew I wasn't paying attention. Well, who could right now?

Besides, Sinclair would give me the scoop on anything I needed to know when we were alone. Meanwhile I, the Daphne of the Undead, had a mystery to solve.

I carefully nudged the car seat with the toe of my left shoe, forcing it farther away from the desk and toward the middle of the floor.

Again, Derik veered. He didn't look down. He didn't frown at the baby, or at me. He just kept giving the sleeping BabyJon a wide berth. And it looked like Jeannie hadn't noticed the phenomenon, which didn't surprise me. She'd just lost a family member; her mind was definitely on other things.

Hmmmm.

"—know when the service will be," Michael was saying.

I was instantly diverted. *Ah ha!* Now we would find out the secret of werewolf funeral rituals. Did they burn the body on a pyre? Loft it into the ocean? Cremate it and scatter the ashes over sacred moss? Bury her while in wolf form with some yowling ritual under the yellow glow of a full moon? Preserve her in spice-soaked cocoon wrappings underground, like mummies?

Everyone was staring at me, and I would have died if I hadn't already. I hate when I think I'm *thinking* something only to find out I've been saying it out loud.

"Pyres?" Michael asked. "Yowling ritual?"

"Oh, fuck me twice," Derik said, throwing his hands in the air. "Did you really think we were going to bury Antonia in the woods like she was a dog treat?"

"Well, how'm I supposed to know what you're going to do?" I snapped back as I leaned over and pulled BabyJon's car seat closer. "That's why we're *here*. To do things *your* way. Ow!" Sinclair had kicked me none too gently in the ankle. I glared at him, then returned my attention to Derik. "Sorry. Muscle spasm."

"Mummies," Derik was muttering. "Funeral pyres. *Burial at sea?* Antonia was Presbyterian, morons."

How anticlimactic.

"You may call me whatever you wish," my husband was saying in a voice more smoke than sound. "But do not insult my wife and queen."

"Well, which is it?" Jeannie asked. I heard the clinking rattle of more ice as she filled her glass with something. Her tone was okay; she didn't sound mean or anything. Sort of half-teasing/half-curious. "Are you here wearing your wife hat or your queen hat?"

Huh. Hope they had a few hours to kill, because it was a long story.

the Antichrist lived in Dinkytown. She was probably right down the block from a Cinnabon chain, too. As Jim Gaffigan said, "Tell me that place isn't run by Satan.").

Anyway, Laura has her own place and I imagine she eats most of her meals there. And since she's alive, she buys food. Which she keeps in her fridge.

Our fridge, nearly big enough to use in a restaurant, is not so lucky. Today its contents revealed four bottles of Diet Peach Snapple (as a doctor, I never touched diet anything . . . why not just drink gasoline and be done with it?), a carton of strawberries (which, as they were not in season, tasted like tiny, fuzzy raw potatoes), two pints of cream, half a box of Godiva truffles (I knew, without looking, that Betsy had already scored the raspberry ones, pureeing them with milk in one of the six blenders), an open box of baking soda that was not doing its job to defunk the fridge, fourteen bottles of water, a near-empty bottle of Thousand Island dressing, a cellophane-wrapped chunk of parmesan cheese so hard it could be used successfully as a blunt instrument, an unopened jar of lemon curd (whatever the hell that was), two cans of Diet Coke (Jessica was addicted to it; why is it that the chronically underweight were drawn to drink diet soda? And am I the only one to notice someone who drank seven cans a day ended up with cancer?), and something foul lurking beneath the tinfoil on a paper plate . . . I just wasn't up to exploring (I didn't even know we had paper plates), so I let it be.

This is what comes of living with vampires and a woman who seems to consume nothing but salads and Diet Coke. Unlike the community fridge, the freezer was full, but still weird. It fairly bulged with bottles of a vodka brand I'd never heard of—Zyr—in various flavors. The flavors were alphabetized. The bottles were perfectly lined up; they were like cloudy glass soldiers at attention.

As these were typical contents of the mansion's kitchen freezer, I knew some of the flavors lurking in the back were lime, juniper, peppercorn, espresso, fennel, mint, garlic, cherry, sun-dried tomato, mustard seed, apple, and horseradish.

Dude, I am not making this up, or exaggerating for humorous effect. In a household of oddities and the undead, Tina was everywhere and nowhere. She excelled at going unnoticed and she could pull that off anywhere in the world . . . except our kitchen freezer. Vodka was her vice; the more obscure the flavor, the more she had to try it. She drank it neat, using a succession of antique shot glasses, which were always kept chilled.

Tina had offered to make me a drink once. I had accepted. Once.

I did not have time to swing by Cub on the way to work and would be too tired after my shift; time to order pizza again. Green Mill was practically on my speed dial.

Sighing, I swung the freezer shut and my senses, instantly overwhelmed by someone they hadn't smelled, seen, or heard, but who was all of a sudden right there, *went into overdrive*. My adrenal gland dumped a gallon of F.O.F. into my system (what my interns called Fight or Flight juice) and for a long minute I thought my heart was going to just quit from the shock.

She greeted me with "I am out of cinnamon vodka," then grabbed my shoulder and prevented me from braining myself on the metal handle as I flinched hard enough to be mistaken for an epileptic.

"Tina," I groaned, yanking my hand out of her chilly grasp, "that's the second time today. I'm putting a bell around your neck. Or sewing one into your scalp, I swear to—" No, don't swear to God;

just hearing the G word was like a whiplash to a vampire. The movies had gotten some things right. "I swear," I finished.

Tina looked mildly distressed. Most of her expressions were mild versions of what humanity could come up with. What would put you or me in a killing rage would cause her to raise one eyebrow and frown. Frown sternly, but still.

The smooth efficiency and profound, almost unshakable calm were at odds with her appearance. Tina looked like an escapee from Delta Nu, the sorority Reese Witherspoon's character made famous in Legally Blonde. (Great movie, dude. "All those opposed to chafing, please say aye.")

Tina had long, honey blond hair—past her shoulders in rippling waves—and big, dark eyes, what Tina called pansy eyes. Tina looked too young to vote; she would probably get carded if she tried to buy cigarettes. And she dressed to play up her appearance in a never-ending variety of kicky plaid skirts, white button-downs, anklets, everything but a backpack full of high school textbooks. She looked like a walking, talking felony. One far older and smarter than any would-be college boy who might try out a little date rape.

Also, she was about as noisy as an unplugged television. If you don't believe that, dude, you couldn't feel my heart just now.

"I apologize, Marc. I honestly don't mean to frighten you." This was true, and scary in its own way—I hated to think what she could do to my nervous system if she really put some thought into it. "We're just two peas rattling around in a can 'round here, aren't we?"

She laughed a little and I noticed she had slipped again. Most of the time, Tina had the smooth, accent-free tones of a weather reporter. But occasionally a Southern accent would creep in. I loved it when that happened because she seemed less a smooth-voiced butler and more like a walking, talking, feeling person.

Don't misunderstand; I have no problem with the undead, although I was dying to learn all I could and trying to work up the nerve to ask Betsy if I could autopsy the next Big Bad she would inadvertently kill with a heretofore unknown superpower. Nope; no real problem with them, I just thought they should get back to their roots a bit more often.

Besides, Tina made me nervous.

And she knew she made me nervous. This was

nothing I could discuss with Betsy, of course . . . my feelings were too vague and unformed and frankly, my best gal wasn't what I would ever call a deep thinker. As Susan Sarandon said in the greatest movie in the history of cinema, Bull Durham, *"The world is made for people who aren't cursed with self-awareness." The world was made, in other words, for people like Betsy.*

She had no time for "Hmm, Tina's a quiet one, huh? Perhaps we should ponder what that signifies," particularly during the fall when she had to update her collection of winter footgear. But it was there and I couldn't deny it: Tina gave me the creeps.

I knew she had been born the year the Civil War had begun.

I knew she had been a vampire long before Sinclair.

I knew she had made Sinclair, had remained by his side all the years since then, and was his capable assistant.

And that was all I knew about her. And I only knew those things because Betsy had told me. In other words, that was all Betsy knew about her, too. And she was *the queen, for the love of . . .*

Dude, there are all sorts of etiquette rules for

living with vampires. There had to be; there was etiquette for everything. But it was hard to come up with a tactful way to ask, "So, how'd you get murdered, anyway?" And that was only one of the things I would love to learn.

All this went through my head in about eleven seconds. Meanwhile, Tina was still lurking—well, standing—by the fridge.

"Will you have a drink with me?" She opened the freezer and reached for the first row of bottles. I saw she had extracted mustard seed–flavored vodka and, thanks to years of seeing man's inhumanity to man via the emergency room, I manfully concealed my shudder.

"I have to get to work," I said glumly.

Curious, I waited a beat, but Tina did exactly what I anticipated. "Oh, that's too bad, Marc. A pity you won't have time to shop first."

Dude, if I had been Sinclair or Betsy, her answer would have been something like, "Oh most wondrous undead monarch, please give me, your humblest, lamest, most slovenly servant, your grocery list and I shall fill your fridge with any produce, meat by-products, Little Debbie snack cakes, and dairy products you desire and also pick up your dry *cleaning* on my way home, unless you would prefer I simply run out to KFC for some original recipe chicken."

Alas, it was not to be: not only was I alive and well, I was neither the vampire queen nor the vampire king. Tina was their *willing and untiring slave,* not mine.

Still, *we* were roommates. You would think that would lead to some kind of bond. The Sacred Roommate Bond. Would it kill her to bring home a gallon of milk once in a while?

Chapter 11

The words *wife* or *queen* seemed almost to hang in the air over our heads. I had the sense that they weren't asking these questions out of idle curiosity, or to be polite. No, no. Michael was a predator, of course, as Antonia had been, which meant he was constantly on the lookout for weakness. He couldn't help it. Probably he didn't even know he was doing it.

Wife or queen? A question I had asked myself on more than one occasion. Sinclair was bigger, stronger, faster. Older. Richer. Better educated. More even-tempered, more in control. Frankly, there were times—lots of times—when I wished I could just be the wife, and leave the whole vamp royalty thing to him.

But I could do things no other vampire on the planet could. Seemed dumb not to take advantage of that, or at least acknowledge it. So we existed in an interesting state of love and respect.

Well, occasional respect, when I wasn't giving him a Wet Willy or poking him in his flat belly when we showered together—the man wasn't ticklish! Talk about an unnatural creature.

He'd bowed to my authority on more than one occasion, too—usually just before I started hurling heavy objects at his head to emphasize whatever point I was making. You want to see something funny? Eric Sinclair, following one of my orders. Believe me, it didn't happen all that often. Whenever it did, he always had an odd expression on his face: part admiration, part annoyance.

Now where the hell was I? Dammit! It was three A.M., I was tired out from being on edge all night, and was having more trouble than usual following the conversation, which had veered from funeral rights to religion to atheist vampires to my title.

"Funny thing for *you* to ask, Jeannie," I finally said. I guess it wasn't exactly unheard of for a werewolf to marry a—you know, a regular person. But it was rare enough so that the two of them caused a stir now and again—I'd gotten that much from Antonia, and that only after she'd been living with us for a while.

Get this: not only was it rare for werewolves to marry boring old humans, it was considered super-lucky for the Pack, and the offspring were usually exceptional Pack members. For example, Antonia—

But I wasn't ready to go there again. Call me a chickenshit coward; that's fine. I just couldn't do it again right now.

"Mmm." Jeannie grinned but didn't rise to the bait, just shrugged. "Good point."

I cleared my throat, because I was having trouble swallowing the whole—the whole mundaneness of the thing. Mundaneness? Mundanity? "So there are Presbyterian werewolves, and Catholic ones, and Lutherans—"

"And Buddhists and atheists and Hindus," Derik added.

"Will you please stop that pacing and sit the fuck down? Ow!" I yanked my poor sore ankle out of reach of Sinclair's foot. "You look like a cheetah on crack."

"Back off, blondie," Derik snapped back and, if anything, sped up the pacing.

"I'm surprised you didn't draw your own conclusion," Michael said loudly, clearly trying to distract us. I think he was clearly trying. It was hard to know *what* the guy was up to. "Because clearly, all vampires are Christians."

"No," Sinclair said.

No? What, no? How did we get off the topic of werewolf retribution for Antonia and on to religion? I got enough of the "let's all pray to Jesus meek and mild" stuff I needed from Laura.

"No?"

"No. We, too, have Muslims and Catholics and pagans. We, too, have—"

"Whoa, whoa, whoa," Jeannie interrupted. "That makes no sense at all."

"We do not go about our lives with the objective of making sense to strangers," my husband said with terrifying pleasantness.

"Fuck." Derik, thank God, had grabbed a chair, dragged it over, turned it so it was facing backward, and sat. His blond hair fell into his eyes and he shook it out of his face with a quick, impatient movement. "Why would a cross work on an atheist vampire?"

Sinclair and I traded a glance. Jessica, I noticed, was all ears as well—she'd been so quiet I'd almost forgotten she was in the room.

"Or someone Jewish?" Derik continued.

Because vampirism was a virus. A virus that was very hard to catch, and even harder to pass on. This was Marc's theory, backed up by Tina and Sinclair— again, not all of a sudden. After months and months and months. Tina and Sinclair couldn't be much more tight-mouthed if someone sewed their lips shut with ultralite fishing line.

Vampirism, as a virus, slowed your metabolism waaaaay down, but didn't stop it. Good points: you no longer sweated, or peed. Aging seemed to stop altogether. You were faster, stronger. Heightened senses. Blah-blah.

Bad points: vampires were highly susceptible to suggestion. (All of them—modest cough—except me.) Tina, my husband's right-hand woman (she had been the one to turn him into a vampire in the early part of the twentieth century . . . yup, I was in love and regularly boinking a man old enough to be my grandfather), had eventually advanced this theory with Marc.

Marc went into MD mode and had tentatively

concurred (on the grounds that he could change his mind if further proof emerged) that yes, it was a virus, and yes, a Jewish vampire would cringe away from a cross. Because we all know that's what vampires do. *They* are vampires; *ergo,* crosses and holy water can hurt them.

I know, sounds stupid, right? Give it a minute. If you catch a disease that makes you highly suggestible, and you have the weight of a zillion horror movies telling you holy water burns . . . then holy water burns.

But we were getting off the point.

And it was driving me so nuts, I was practically biting the tip of my tongue off so I wouldn't point out that Derik had made the same silly assumptions about vampires that we had about werewolves. After calling us morons.

"—explain what happened?"

Eh? Aw, shit. Michael was looking right at me. I jerked my foot away in time and Sinclair's Kenneth Cole–shod shoe clunked into the back of Michael's desk.

"Explain what happened?" I repeated with what I hoped was an intelligent question on my face.

"Yes, to the Council."

Council? What council? That didn't sound good at all. Nobody had said anything about a council—I think. Damn. I really should be paying attention to the goings-on in my life. "Can't *you* tell them what happened? You're the boss around here."

"No." Click. Closed. End of argument. I knew that tone—I'd heard it in my husband's voice often enough to know when it was no good to protest. "We'll be meeting on the grounds just after sunset tomorrow. I'll need all of your testimonies, so do not send one representative to speak for the group.

"Then what?" I asked nervously.

He just looked at me, almost like he was sorry for me.

Somehow, that was even worse than his cool fury.

Chapter 12

Dude,

Here I am again, shift over (and I managed to leave the hospital on time, a miracle of parting-the-Red-Sea proportion), writing the day after Betsy and the others flew away to Cape Cod to face whatever music there was to face. I'd asked to go and had been gently refused. Jessica got to go, but then, it was her airplane.

That left Tina—as I mentioned earlier, she was a sort of supersecretary to Sinclair—and Laura and me.

I didn't have a chance to go into Laura much before I had to leave for work (and grocery *shopping). Now I've got some time and, as it's day-time, Tina won't be lurking in a shadowy corner of the kitchen, waiting to startle me to death before smoothly apologizing.*

So. Laura. A word or two about her, yes, please. Very, very nice girl. Young . . . not even drinking age. She studied hard at the U of M and was a credit to her parents. Excellent health, and conventionally beautiful if you liked slender, fair-skinned blondes with terrific breasts, long legs, and big blue eyes.

She was also occasionally homicidal and cursed (or was it more of an inheritance?) with an unbelievably bad temper. When she's upset about something, you can practically feel the air get heavier and warmer. One thing I hated to see was Laura's hair shading from buttercup yellow to auburn, as it always did when she was infuriated.

According to the Book of the Dead, a sort of vampire bible, Laura is fated to destroy us all, something Betsy seems to keep overlooking or forgetting. Or forgetting on purpose (she's not quite the ditz she'd like us to believe . . . at least I think she isn't).

A digression for a minute: the Book of the Dead was kept in the mansion's library, on its own stand. Betsy didn't talk about it much, but she practically babbled about it nonstop compared to how much Tina and Sinclair discussed it. So you can imagine how frustrating it was to get just a minor detail or two about the vampire bible.

It was bound in human skin, and written in blood by a crazy vampire a thousand years ago. Everything in it (so far) came true. And (here comes the fun part!) anyone who read it too long went clinically insane. Scariest of all, Betsy had tried to destroy it— twice—and it always found its way back to her.

I wasn't dumb enough to try to read it, but I did want a look at it. I waited for a night when I had the mansion to myself (Betsy and the others were off trying to catch a serial killer—or maybe it was the time that crooked cop set the Fiends free? Who could keep track of their nocturnal crime-fighting habits? Well, it doesn't matter now.), then went into the library.

I didn't sneak. I live here, too. I was not sneaking, nor being a sneak. I walked. I walked right up to the stand. I reached out a hand. I wasn't going to read it. I wasn't. I just wanted to—

Wait.

* * *

Okay, I'm back. I had to take a second and go throw up. Which is what I did those few months ago when I grasped the cover to flip the book open. I didn't even get a good look at the title page, never mind the table of contents, before I started vomiting blood.

As a doctor, I found this to be a somewhat alarming symptom, especially since I had felt perfectly fine ten seconds earlier. I made it to the nearest bathroom—thank goodness the mansion's got about thirty of them!—and, between bouts, called my friend Marty (part-time EMT, full-time guy who could keep his mouth shut) for a ride to the hospital.

By the time he got me there, I was fine again. His backseat was a mess, though. It cost me six hundred bucks to get it clean again.

Sorry, dude, that was a major digression, not a minor one. So that's enough about the vampire bible, which I now prudently stay the holy hell away from; let's get back to Laura.

It's hard to believe that a gorgeous sweet Norwegian is the Antichrist. And even harder to imagine her destroying a cactus plant, much less the entire world. When she's blond, anyway.

When Betsy and Laura first hooked up, we had no idea she even had a dark side (which was silly . . . don't we all?). Then she killed a serial killer. And then she beat a vampire almost to death. More worrisome was the fact that she could have done much, much worse. Because Laura's weapons pop out of nowhere when she's mad, and they show up express delivery from hell.

And lately she's been skipping church. She'd already been over here twice, and Betsy hasn't been out of the state even twenty-four hours. I think she's lonesome. Scratch that—I was familiar with all the symptoms. I knew Laura was lonesome.

I also knew she was extremely dangerous. But I know better than to try to open a dialogue with her about the subject. Laura hated her birthright, her heritage, her mother. Hated knowing someone had predicted she'd destroy the world almost a thousand years before she was born. I was pretty sure she hated the fact that we all knew about it, too.

So. Tonight we're going out for drinks, and I'll tease her and we'll gossip about Betsy and Co. at the nearest smoothie bar and then Laura will be herself again.

For a while.

Chapter 13

The last thing we did before going to bed was set up Sinclair's laptop—

Right, Sinclair, I forgot to explain that. I hardly ever call him Eric. He's always been Sinclair to me (or Sink Lair, when he's really pissing me off), just as I have always been Elizabeth (yech!) to him. I still can't believe my mother stuck me with a first name like Elizabeth when *my last name was Taylor.* What, did she lose a bet?

Anyway, I was Betsy to everyone except the man I loved.

And speaking of the man I loved, he was rapidly typing something, probably an update e-mail to

Tina. Then he showed me one of Marc's typically annoying e-mails, which went like this:

> *Hey, girrrrl! miss you guys already, i mean WTF? Hope the furry friends haven't eaten any of you yet, LOL! love, marc*

Oh, boy. Don't even get me started.

Too late, I'm starting. What the hell was it about e-mail that made everybody forget the stuff they learned in second grade, like capitalizing *I* and proper names, and using periods? Hello? We all learned how to do this less than five years out of diapers!

And what was with all the increasingly stupid acronyms? Nobody with any sense would dare send out a snail-mail letter written in that odd, juvenile style. No one would send a business letter written like that. But I've seen executive VPs send out e-mails riddled with spelling and punctuation errors and LOLs.

Somehow, when I wasn't looking, and because it's electronic mail, none of the basic grammar rules applied.

Barf.

Sinclair obligingly vacated the desk chair for me.

I plopped into it and kicked off my pumps. However the werewolves might feel about us, they were pretty good hosts so far. This was the most beautiful bedroom I'd ever seen. No, not bedroom . . . suite. A sitting room. An office. A teeny kitchen. Two bathrooms. A living room with a piano in the corner. A freaking piano, who lives like this? And a bed so gigantic I felt as small as a saltine cracker when I lay on it.

I clicked on REPLY and rapidly typed.

Marc, you nitwit, how many times do I have to tell you, enough with the acronyms. I'm assuming since you made it through college and medical school that sometime before you left for college someone mentioned a cool new invention: punctuation. Try it sometime. You might like it.

Clicked on SEND. Stretched in the chair like a cat, then got up and ambled over to my husband, who held his arms out to me. He was smiling his sexy, somehow sweet smile and I could see the light glinting off his fangs, teeth so sharp they made a rattlesnake seem like it had a mouthful of rubber bands.

I grinned back, kicked out of my clothes, and

pulled the sheet back. As my husband's fangs sank into my neck and things began to go dark and sweet around the edges of my brain, I had a thought: *What about werewolf hearing?* Shit on that, how about their sense of smell, which was even better than a vampire's? Even if they couldn't hear us, they could sure tell what we were doing.

Then Eric's fingers were gently parting my thighs and stroking me in that luscious, insistent way he knew I loved, and I forgot all about werewolf hearing. Hell, I'd be lucky if I didn't forget my own name.

Chapter 14

Dude!

You will not *believe this. I was there, and I almost don't believe it. And there's no way to pretty this up, so I'm just going to spell it straight out: a group of Satan worshippers found Laura.*

Yes! And yes, I know how it sounds! But it's all true; my God, I can hardly type I'm so excited/freaked out/amazed.

Okay, so this is what happened. Laura called and asked if she could hang out at the mansion, and of course I said yes. It was daytime, so Tina was snoring away somewhere (not that she snored, or even breathed, but you know what I mean). So into the mansion I come, only to be greeted by a scene out of—of—shit, I have no frame of reference for this.

Real Satanists had apparently tracked Laura down via astrology (not my field, so much of the explanation I got later went right over my head). Apparently, just as there was a star of Bethlehem, there is also a Morningstar, which shows up just before the Antichrist comes into her maturity.

?????

Seriously, dude, I know how it sounds. A star? Laura's own star, shining down on the planet like a treasure map leading Satanists to our door? (And why not her apartment? Why Betsy's place?) A star that didn't show until her maturity, what the hell did that mean? The star didn't show itself until she had a driver's license? A passport? Until she was legal drinking age? What?

Laura either didn't know or wasn't saying— pardon me while I evince a complete lack of surprise. And I suppose it doesn't matter. What matters is the star is here (I plan to dip into my savings first thing tomorrow and buy a decent telescope to set up in the yard . . . I simply have to see this puppy for myself), as well as people who have read the *right books and worshipped the right demon and made the right sacrifices. (I'm guessing on that last one, but the movies can't be all wrong, right? Memo to me: Netflix* Rosemary's Baby.*)*

Anyway, the right people can now track Laura down pretty much at will.

Which is why, when I walked into the house after a milk run, I nearly tripped over the dozen people kneeling in front of Laura, who was blushing like a tomato. A demonic tomato. I was instantly alarmed; she was so fire-hydrant red, so incredibly flushed, I was afraid she was going to stroke out, and I almost dropped the milk.

They had (not on purpose, I'm sure of that) backed Laura into a corner of the kitchen and were moaning and praying.

Yeah. Praying. Praying to Laura.

I don't know what I should do with this information, not to mention the stuff that happened afterward. Betsy has enough on her plate these days. And it wasn't like Laura had killed anybody.

In fact, the way she handled it was nothing short of hilarious. She—

Wait. She's calling me from the hallway. More later, dude.

Chapter 15

When I next opened my eyes, it was, according to the grandfather clock bonging away at the other end of our suite, four o'clock. Our bedroom was utterly gloomy, thanks to all the heavy curtains, so I stretched and sat up, swung my legs over the bed, and thought about what to do.

Sinclair was still—ha, ha—dead to the world beside me. He was on his side, one arm flung out, palm up. His normally pin-neat hair was a ruffled dark mass; his lips were slightly parted.

I watched his chest for a long time . . . three minutes, almost. I think it rose once. But he felt like living flesh; he was warm (we're speaking comparably, of course). He wasn't a corpse, he wasn't dead. He wasn't alive, either.

Undead.

Stupid word, I've always hated that word.

This was the part of every day when I deeply pitied my husband, and I would never tell him. Sinclair needed me for several things—pity wasn't one of them. He didn't have to sleep all day, and he could stay awake when the sun came up (unlike yours truly, who would drop like a puppet with her strings cut as soon as it was dawn) but he could never, ever go out into the sun.

I, however, could.

So I got to my feet and checked on BabyJon, who we'd set up in the small sitting room. And by the way? The guy who invented the port-a-crib? A genius of Jonas Salk proportions.

Anyway, he was in his crib, flat on his back with his little arms in the "this is the police, put your hands up" position. If he grew up to be anything like the Ant, he couldn't practice that position soon enough.

I couldn't help but smile when I looked at him. Don't get me wrong, it was unfortunate that my father and his wife died. But BabyJon was mine now.

Forever.

Best of all, he was adjusting to the new sleeping schedule. After all, I can't have a kid running around during the day when I sleep. No, BabyJon was officially on graveyard shift now, and for a long time to come.

I wondered what I would tell him when he was older. *"Mom, why is there an unconscious man stuffed in the closet?"*

"Nothing to worry about, dear, Mommy just wanted a snack."

Hmm. Better rethink that one. Later. Besides, since he'd be growing up with us, he'd probably think it's normal for parents to stay up all night and never eat solid food. Or age. Or poop.

A problem for another time, so I popped into the bathroom, which was more or less unnecessary, but old habits, right? Sometime during our late-night chat with the Wyndhams, a castle employee had unpacked our clothes and stocked the bathroom. Good stuff, too—Aveda products.

Feeling minty fresh, I left the bathroom, and pulled on brown velvet leggings and a long-sleeved blue flannel shirt. I was always cold, and had long since donated all my tank tops to Goodwill. I slipped into my Cole Haan Penny Air Loafers and was ready to face the day. What was left of it, anyway.

I had to walk through the rest of the suite, and after a second I realized that our suite was on the west side of the castle. Okay, mansion—really huge, amazing mansion. That looked, to my Midwestern eyes, awfully like a castle.

Someone was being pretty thoughtful. Never let it be said that werewolves weren't polite hosts—I only had to look around our guest suite to see that. But I drew all the curtains anyway, just to be on the safe side. I didn't want to take the smallest chance that Sinclair might get burned. The sun wouldn't go down for another four hours or so.

I stepped out into the hallway, pulled the door closed, and nearly fell over Jessica, who was all but lurking in the doorway of the suite directly across from ours.

"You know, they did let you have that room," I said. "In fact, I think they're assuming you'll use it, as opposed to lingering in strange hallways."

She responded to me with, "Girl, I am bored outta my tits."

"Can we have one cross-country quest without talking about your tits?"

Her pretty dark eyes went narrow and thoughtful,

and she caressed her cheek with a long fingernail colored jack-o'-lantern orange. After a thoughtful pause, she shook her head. "I don't see how."

"I figured." I scanned the hallway and listened hard: it was as empty as it looked. "Want to find the kitchen? Maybe whip up a—"

"If I have to look at another smoothie this month, I'm going to barf in one of your Beverly Feldmans."

"And face a terrible, prolonged death." We fell in step and, when we reached the main staircase, I pointed in the direction of the kitchen—or whatever room smelled like spices, meat, and fresh vegetables.

"How can you be bored in the middle of a Pack of werewolves?"

"Easy. They're not talking to me. The ones I bump into are soooo polite—bathroom's right there, the east wing's over there, one of the indoor pools is through there, the weight room is over there—but I'm a cipher here."

Jessica, well used to my blank expression, correctly interpreted it as "I am unfamiliar with that word; please explain" and added, "I'm a nobody. A nothing. A zero. This is about vampires and werewolves, which, thank God, I'm neither. No offense."

"Who could be offended by that?" I muttered, jumping down the last four steps. "That way. Then a right. So, they've been nice to you at least?"

"Sure."

"Good. Listen, I think it's really good that you're here—"

"You're the worst liar in the galaxy."

"Shut up. Anyway, I sort of forced BabyJon on Sinclair—"

"This I already knew. The entire street knew," she added thoughtfully.

"—because we're his parents now and we have to learn how to be a family—"

"Uh-huh, yup. Getting to something I *don't* know anytime soon?"

"—but I can't watch him every minute I'm here."

"I don't mind watching him—much—but you know he'll only be cute and cuddly with you. With me . . ." She sighed. "With everybody else, it's colic city."

"Sorry, Jess. I can't help that. But I appreciate you watching out for him for me."

She waved it away, and obediently turned left when I pointed. We were now in a slightly narrower hallway, on hardwood floors this time, no carpet. The smell of food was *very* strong.

"At least you got the boy trained. Sleeps half the day *and* half the night."

"He's really very sweet," I whined.

Jessica snorted and straight-armed the swinging door into the kitchen.

Like everything, the Wyndham kitchen made mine look like a dining nook. At least four big tables—the kind you could chop anything on—with long legs. Another big table, marble-topped, probably for baking. Three fridges. Another door, which led to industrial-sized freezers. I could smell the Freon.

There were huge windows—one overlooking a kitchen garden—on every wall. The windows on the opposite wall overlooked the Atlantic.

"I could get used to this," Jessica commented.

"So buy something just like it. You've probably got enough money in the sofa cushions for a down payment."

Jessica shrugged and went to the nearest fridge while I slid onto a bar stool. "I like the place in St. Paul."

I nodded. Shoot, before the mansion, she'd lived in an ordinary house in the suburbs. She had never lived rich, dressed rich, ate rich, or looked rich. It was one of her many charms.

"So you're not, um, hungry, are you?" Jessica had extracted an apple and a Diet Coke. Wait'll I rat her out to Marc! He considered diet pop one step up from muriatic acid, whatever the hell that was.

"Naw. Sinclair and I snacked on each other for a while last night. I'm good for a few days."

"Good to know. If you go nuts and accidentally chew on one of the locals—"

"Right, I get the picture, and *duh*, like I haven't thought of that. How dumb do you think I am?"

Her answer was muffled in the loud crunch as she went to work on the apple . . . probably just as well.

"So, that Jeannie seems nice," Jessica said, masticating slowly.

"Shhhh," I said, putting a finger to my lips.

Jessica gnawed and crunched and all but growled at her McIntosh for a good minute, when the doors swung inward (werewolves must just *know* if someone's on the other side; probably because they could smell them) and in walked Jeannie, carrying a toddler, and behind her, Lara.

"Hello," Jeannie said. The toddler, a boy with his mother's wild blond curls and blue eyes, waved a chubby hand in our general direction. "Sleep all right?"

"Like the dead," I said cheerfully.

Jeannie rolled her eyes at me in a remarkable imitation of Jessica. She carefully set the toddler down in a high chair, strapped him in, then started rooting around for toddler food.

"Mmmmph gmmmph mmmm nughump mph," Jessica commented, tiny pieces of apple flying like shrapnel.

"She didn't know you had another kid." Or forgot Jeannie had another kid . . . she'd been a little out of it when the Wyndhams visited us the last time. Chemo really plays havoc with your memory.

"This? This is Sean. And you remember Lara, Betsy."

"Hullo," the tiny werewolf said as she opened the fridge, pulling out a small Tupperware bowl. She popped the lid, and—

"Don't you *dare*," Jeannie said severely, pretending not to hear the delicate sound of Jessica's gagging. "You have one of the chefs cook that hamburger, or ask me to."

"But it tastes better when it's raw," Lara the Weird whined.

"You heard what I said." Jeannie plunked a Lunchable in front of her son, who carefully began dismantling it and eating.

"But I *want* to eat a raw hamburger."

Jessica raised her eyebrows at me while Lara placed her teeny hands on her teeny hips and glared up at her mother.

"Tough nuts," Jeannie replied with admirable unconcern. "And that locked gaze might work with your father and the others, but it doesn't do diddly to me. So: Cooked hamburger? Or no hamburger?"

"No hamburger."

"Ah, starving yourself to spite the woman who gave you life." Jeannie leaned against the counter and put a hand over her eyes. "Ah, 'how sharper than a serpent's tooth it is to have a thankless child.'"

"Mommy Shakes," Sean said, carefully picking up a pepperoni slice and popping it into his mouth.

"Yes, that's right, Mommy likes to quote Shakespeare."

Lara sighed. "Since I'm not going to eat my snack, can I go to the playground?"

"Lara, I'm sorry, but I can't get away right now—

your father and I have some stuff to talk about." Her gaze slid to me, but I don't think she was aware of it.

"I'll take her," I volunteered. "I'd like to get outside."

"Oh. Well. That's very nice, Betsy, but you're not really used to werewolves, y'see, and—"

"Not used to— Hello? I lived with one of them?"

Jeannie gave me a long, speculative look, then beckoned with one finger. "Step over here with me for a moment. Would you?"

Jessica shot me her you'd-better-tell-me-every-thing-later expression and added, "I'll keep an eye on your boy for you, Jeannie."

"That's great, Jessica. If he wants another Lunchable—"

"And he will," Lara piped up.

"—they're on the bottom shelf in the fridge to your right."

So saying, she spun on her heel and walked out through a different door, one I hadn't even spotted until Jeannie moved toward it.

I guess I was going back down the rabbit hole. Me and Alice.

Chapter 16

I'll trust you with my daughter," Jeannie began the moment she'd started up four washing machines at once. The mysterious door had led to the mysterious Laundromat. The Wyndhams had their own Laundromat! Unreal.

Anyway, she got a bunch of the machines going and I was puzzling over that when I suddenly realized: she didn't want Lara to overhear. Or anybody close by to overhear.

"I'm doing this," she continued, "because I know you liked Antonia and wouldn't have seen her dead. I'm also doing this because Lara can take care of herself. So if you turn evil and try to bite her or hurt her in any way, don't be surprised if it's your head bouncing across the playground."

"That's, um, sweet. You must be very proud."

"But I need you to remember this: a werewolf cub is not a human child. They're different."

"Okay."

"They're faster. Stronger. Even crueler. She looks like a little girl to you, but you must never forget—she is her father's daughter, the man who had to kill over twenty-five werewolves to take the Pack. Do you understand?"

I just stared at her while all around us washing machines went *shhh-thump, shhh-thump, shhh-thump.*

I'd expected the standard warning: if you bite my kid, I'll hunt you down and shoot you dead.

But it wasn't like that. Jeannie wasn't scared for Lara.

She was scared for *me.*

"I told you something like this before, but you had a lot going on at the time. This time I've got your full attention. Right?"

"Right, absolutely, you bet."

"As long as we understand each other."

"Oh, we totally do," I assured her.

"All right, then."

"All right."

Chapter 17

With her warning still ringing in my ears, we trooped back to the kitchen after Jeannie opened one of the dryers, groped around inside, then turned the dryer back on. "A quilt," she explained, and I nodded just like this was an ordinary week, day, conversation, whatever.

We got back just in time to hear Lara laughing and Jessica's "Ooof! All right, all right, you crummy kid, you win the bet."

Jessica, obviously the loser in a game of arm wrestling, looked relieved to see me as she rubbed her shoulder. "Ah, the Mysterioso Twins are back. What's up?"

"Just giving her directions to the playground," Jeannie calmly lied. "Lara, you can go, but you mind Betsy like it was me talking—you understand?"

"Yes, Mom." Lara slid off the stool and faced me.

"Hi again," the next Pack leader said.

"Nice pigtails," I replied.

Chapter 18

That was how I found myself taking Lara— Michael and Jeannie's eldest—to the nearby playground for good, clean, wholesome werewolf fun.

She was a cutie, no question. She had her father's eyes, that odd yellow-gold I'd seen on television nature shows—eyes the color of an owl's, or a hawk's. Slender and straight, with her curly dark hair pulled into pigtails. Jeans and a Hannah Montana T-shirt. Maybe . . . six?

"—then Daddy said you were going to bring Antonia back but now you have to talk to the Council and nobody knows what will happen after that but Derik's really upset because he loves—loved—Antonia and—"

"Where the hell is the playground?" I muttered. Lara, as far as I could tell, hadn't taken a breath in the last eight minutes. We'd taken a path that led off the grounds and onto a small, brick-lined sidewalk beside a bike trail. Lara had explained that it was "really close." Sure it was.

"—had to go before the Council since Grandpa took over the Pack so nobody knows what's going to—"

"There *is* no park," I muttered. "That's my theory. I'm trapped on a never-ending sidewalk beside a never-ending bike path."

"—walk around outside?"

"What?"

"I said, how come you can come outside? It's daytime."

"I just can."

"But how come?"

It sounded too dumb to say it out loud, but I did it anyway. "Because I'm the queen. Sunlight can't hurt me. Only a knockoff shoe sale can hurt me."

"Because I thought you'd have to sleep in a coffin

but my friend said you guys have one of the guest suites and there's no coffins in there and—"

I stopped. Lara halted beside me. We'd rounded a tree-lined corner and suddenly the park was spread out before us. There was a large sign at the entrance that read, MICHAEL WYNDHAM SR. MEMORIAL PARK.

"Don't tell me," I said. "Let me guess."

"You don't have to guess," Lara said, giving me a look I knew well. It was the what-kind-of-moron-are-you look. "The sign's right there."

"So your dad made this?"

"No. Daddy's the third."

"He's what?"

"Michael Wyndham the Third. My great-grandpa was—"

"You know what? I've kind of lost interest by now." Legacies. I should have remembered where I was. This was New England, not Minnesota. "Run along."

So she did, heading straight for the monkey bars. There weren't many cars in the small parking lot to the left—maybe half a dozen—and about that many kids playing. A couple of moms were sitting on benches on the far side of the park, chatting and keeping half an eye on the children.

Which left me time to think about just what the hell we were in for. For example, just what the hell was the Council? Was it as bad as it sounded? Because it *sounded* a bit like a trial without a jury. Or a fair-minded judge. And what was I supposed to tell them? I hadn't made Antonia take slugs for me, or even asked her to. We walked in, the bad guy shot, and Antonia died. The end.

I prowled around the teeter-totters and tried to think of a plan. But I had no gift for strategy—I left that shit strictly to Sinclair and Tina—and felt more out of my depth than usual. What were we doing here, anyway?

Let's say the Council decided the vampires had screwed up. What then? They couldn't punish us. Could they? Would that mean we'd go to war? That could be a problem—not only did I not know how many vampires were walking around on the planet, I had no way to mobilize them. And I didn't want to. I found it completely ridiculous that I had to police adults, most of whom were far, far older than I was. And as far as siccing them on werewolves, for crying out loud? Puh-leeze.

I kicked irritably at an errant tuft of grass, then looked up at the unmistakable sound of a child bursting into tears. A little girl—three? four?—was sprawled in the gravel, sobbing, and a bigger boy—nine, ten?—was standing over her.

"I said your turn was over," the brat said, sounding remarkably unrepentant. I knew a few vampires like that.

The thing about being childless (as I still thought of myself, BabyJon being a relatively late arrival in my life) is you sort of freeze up when kids are acting badly. On the one hand, you know the kid's in the wrong and you want to help. On the other hand, it's not *your* kid, so perhaps it was none of your business.

The little girl was still crying. The bigger boy was now on her recently vacated swing.

I glanced over at the moms sitting on the bench and saw one stop in mid-gossip and say in that fake "I'm trying to sound stern but I'm really proud of my big boy!" tone that I absolutely hated, "Jaaaaason! You know you're supposed to wait your turn, honey."

"I'm telling!" the tiny girl in the gravel sobbed. "I'm *telling*! Mom! Mommy, Jason pushed me off the—"

"You be nice to your little sister, Jason Dunheim?"

the mom asked. Asked. Not told. Oh, God save me from overindulgent nitwits who insist on procreating but not parenting. "Jason? Okay?"

Why is she *asking*? I hate when parents ask. What happens if the kid says no? Then what are you supposed to do? Slink away? Have a tantrum? What?

"Mommy!"

"Shut up, bawl baby."

"Jason? You know we don't use that phrase in our house, Jason? Honey?"

Sigh. Well, the little one didn't appear to be hurt (I couldn't smell any blood on her), and if I didn't exactly approve of a mother who so clearly favored one child over the other, there wasn't much I—

"Say you're sorry."

I turned my head so fast I nearly gave myself whiplash. Not only was Lara in it (groan), she was hoisting Jason by bunching his T-shirt in her fist.

Chapter 19

Lara lifted his big butt right off the swing, and was holding him a foot over her head with one arm. I'd never even heard her move, and the monkey bars were all the way across the playground from the swings.

"Let go of me!" Jason's legs swung and kicked.

Lara gave him a brisk shake. It looked about as difficult for her as salting pasta would be for me. "Say you're sorry."

"Hey!" Miracle of miracles, The Thing That Spawned Jason was on her feet and running for the swings. "Leave my son alone! Put him down right now!"

I started to run, too. But my motives were in no way altruistic . . . I sure wasn't at all interested in saving Jason's spoiled little white-bread butt.

No, all I could think as I raced toward them was, *First I get Antonia killed, and now I'm going to get Lara beat up . . . Oh, the werewolves are gonna throw us a party, they'll be so pleased. Nice, Betsy. And it's not even five o'clock.*

I made myself slow down. A lot. Because about the only way this could get worse was if I outed myself as a vampire. Humans could not run at forty miles an hour. *Slow down. A lot. Get Lara away from there before she—*

"She's littler than you." Another shake. "And not as strong." Another shake—sort of like when a terrier kills a rat.

Jason had both his hands locked around her wrist and, from his strained, reddening complexion, was trying as hard as he could to pry her hand off him. "You're supposed to watch out for her," Lara the Terrifying was saying. "She's your 'sponsibility and you hurt her on purpose! You don't ever do that!"

"Put me *down*!"

" 'kay." I didn't even have time to groan and cover my eyes; Lara pulled Jason toward her, sidestepped, and threw him about six feet. He skidded nose-first into the gravel, sat up, and started howling. His nose was bleeding and the rich, heady scent went straight to my head.

Well, this was just swell. On top of everything else, I'd popped my fangs. Way to stay off the radar, Vampire Queen.

I reached Lara, veering around the mother who had instantly rushed to her son's side when things stopped going his way.

"Argh, Lara, thith ith awful! Why'd you do that? You can't be throwing bullieth around like that. Are you *trying* to get me eaten alive? Your father—"

Lara was ignoring me. I had, in fact, stopped existing for her at all. She had gone to the girl, helped her out of the dirt, and brushed her off. "Are you okay? We have Band-Aids at my house. Do you need one?"

"Nuh-uh." The girl rubbed her cheeks with grubby fists, mixing dirt with tears. "How'd you do that? That was really cool. I want to do that. Can you throw him again?"

"I better not," Lara muttered, giving me a wary look. Not like she was scared of me; more like she was calculating how much of a threat I was to her at that moment.

I had a flashback to what her mother—her human mother—had told me earlier.

A werewolf cub is not a human child. And what else had she said? She'd looked so strange when she said it. That look on her face—a mixture of pride and sorrow. It wasn't an expression I'd ever seen before.

They're faster. Stronger . . . crueler.

Jeannie had known her shit; Lara was no more human than I was. She hadn't responded to Jason like a little girl who wanted to play on the monkey bars; she'd responded like an alpha who saw weakness and pain and instantly acted to put an end to it. She'd seen someone who needed protecting and she hadn't hesitated—never mind the consequences to her, or me.

Which was a lot more than I had done.

Great. Shown up by someone who didn't weigh more than a bag of dog chow. Who was already more of a leader than I could ever be.

"—because we could go up to my house and—"

"You!" Oh, terrific. The Thing That Birthed Bullies had marched over to us, dragging her bawling son behind her. "You think I didn't see what you did? I saw what you did, and you're going to—"

Okay, that was just about enough. I locked gazes with her and said, "Go thit down."

The anger—all animation, in fact—left her face and she turned and walked like a robot over to the bench. Good old vampire mojo; there were times when I was more than pleased to use it.

"What's wrong with your voice?" Lara asked.

"You jutht never mind my voith. Letth get out of here."

"Hey, your teeth are all pointy! I don't think you should bite him, though." She looked at Jason, who was so bewildered by the events of the last twenty seconds he had stopped crying. Then she smiled at him, the flat, fake smile of a store mannequin. "He wouldn't taste good at all."

Jason was now backing away from her, wiping the blood from his nose with a swipe of his sleeve. I couldn't say I blamed him. And the farther away he got, the less crazy the smell of his O-positive goodness made me.

"Your mom underplayed it, if anything," I muttered.

"What?"

"Never mind. Let's get out of here."

"Okay. I've got what I wanted, anyway."

We started heading out of the playground, back toward Lara's house. "What, you wanted to throw a bully fifteen feet?"

"It wasn't even close to fifteen feet. Boy, you really like to exaggerate, don't you?"

"It's one of my weaknesses," I admitted.

"Besides, I just wanted to get another look at you."

I stopped so suddenly she took a couple more steps before she realized she was walking alone. "You wanted to *what*?"

"To get another look at you. If you and my daddy become enemies, you'll be my enemy. I might have to kill you someday, to protect the Pack. Why wouldn't I come see you?"

"But you and I met already."

"Yes," Lara explained patiently, "but now you're in my lands. I'm not in yours."

I stared, struck speechless—which is not a normal thing for me, better believe it. "So, if I've got this right, you didn't want me to take you to play. You wanted to—to—"

A werewolf cub is not a human child.

"—to size me up?"

"Uh-huh." She brightened as the mansion came into sight. "D'you want some ice cream? I'd love a dish of chocolate."

Okay. Now I was getting a genuine case of the creeps. Because I could see that, for her, the situation was over, done, resolved. She could move on to other things now, and would.

In other words, she was behaving exactly like she was taught and bred to behave: to worry only about the Now. Tomorrow was a thousand years away. Yesterday was even further away.

I sighed and surrendered. "Yeah. Let's go get some ice cream."

"Hey! You're not talking funny anymore."

"Let's thank God for small favors, okay? Also, if you could not mention this little fracas to your folks, that would be peachy."

Lara laughed. "You're funny."

"Yeah, yeah." I followed her up the drive to the mansion. "I'm a barrel of freakin' monkeys."

Chapter 20

Dude,

Well, I definitely picked the right time to keep a journal. Because it has been an interesting couple of days. Who knows? I might actually keep writing the thing.

When Laura called me away during my last entry, I had followed her into the kitchen. But not as her friend . . . I was more than a little alarmed at the symptoms of intense stress she was exhibiting. Since unpleasant things had a way of happening when she was angry or frightened, I had a more than passing interest in her state of mind.

I was able to sit her down at the kitchen table

and get her to drink a Snapple. The act of doing something nice and mundane seemed to calm her. That's when I realized she was more humiliated than angry.

"Marc, I am so sorry you had to see that. I just don't know what to say."

"Laura, it's not your fault. Hey," I joked, "how do you think I'd feel if my old man showed up? You shouldn't feel bad about something beyond your control."

"Maybe it isn't beyond my control."

I wasn't sure I liked the sound of that. "It's fine, Laura, I don't mind. Satanists showing up in the foyer certainly add some spice to my day. Nobody likes the pop-in. And like I said, it's not your fault."

"No. It's my mother's." That last was practically spit out. "I was going to ask you something and now I can't, because of her."

"Ask me what? Drink your tea. So. Ask."

"Um." Laura gazed into her bottle of Snapple, which I doubt held any answers. "It's just, I told Betsy I'd look after you and Tina while she was gone. So instead of coming over when I can, I was hoping I could move in. Just for a little while," she added, misreading my expression. "I won't get in the way, I promise."

"How could you get in the way? There are twenty bedrooms in this thing. But come on, Laura. Cut the bullshit."

"I don't—"

"Betsy asked you to look over Tina, too?"

"Well." Laura looked down for a moment. "Mostly you, I guess. I think she felt bad about leaving you behind."

I shrugged. "It's moot. I didn't have the vacation time, anyway. Tina had to stay, too—somebody's got to stay in Vampire Central and handle any undead-related stuff that comes up while they're gone. Which leaves thee and me. And of course you can move in. Heck, pick an entire wing to live in."

"No, I can't, now." Her knuckles whitened on the bottle. "Not with these—these people tracking me down all the time and asking—"

"Wait. This has happened before?"

Laura didn't say anything. She didn't have to. The Snapple bottle shattered in her hand, spraying tea and glass all over the place.

"Oh my God! I'm sorry, Marc, I didn't mean to be so clumsy, I'll get a towel and—"

I was instantly on my feet, hauled her to hers, and hustled her over to the sink. "Laura, if you don't mellow out, I'm going to slip some Valium into your next Frappuccino. Now hold still and let me look."

I carefully examined her hand, rinsed it, and examined it again. She had a couple of minor cuts on the pads of her left ring and middle fingers, and that was all. Nothing arterial, no damage to the tendons that I could see.

"No more Snapple for you," I said, handing her a dish towel and stepping around the broken glass. "From now on it's strictly sippy cups."

The only reason I was letting her clean up was because it was the only thing that would make her feel better. Laura was nice—a little too nice. She always made me wonder when she was going to blow. Looked like this might be the week.

"You said this has happened before?"

"Yes." She wiped up glass and tea, being careful to get even the smallest pieces. "Those people. They always find me. Always."

"So they show up at your apartment, too?"

"My apartment. My parents' house."

"I'll bet the minister loved that," I said dryly, earning a ghost of a smile. "What do they want with you?"

"To serve me," she replied shortly, wringing the now-wet towel over the sink (after she'd shaken the glass into the garbage).

"Serve you, what? With toast?"

A real smile this time. "No, silly. To do my bidding."

"So what have you done in the past?"

"I just tell them to go away."

"No, no, no."

Laura blinked. "No?"

"You're going about it all wrong."

"I am?"

"It's going to happen anyway, right? Because of that star or whatever heralding you like—I dunno—like January heralds weight-loss resolutions."

"Yes, I suppose." Laura was looking increasingly mystified, which was a big improvement over mortified. "But what else could I do?"

"Lots of things."

Then I told her. And got another smile, this one even better than the last one. This *was* a smile of absolute delight.

Chapter 21

I got back in time to change into a black suit, black panty hose, and Carolina Herrera black pumps. Sinclair was up and working at the desk in our suite; he was also dressed for the service.

Yes, indeed, my first werewolf funeral.

I watched my husband work for a minute until he felt my gaze and turned. "Something on your mind, dear one?"

"Several things," I replied, thinking of Lara, future psycho werewolf leader. "Mostly about how awkward this is going to be. I mean, everyone there will know. They'll know Antonia died saving me."

"I imagine they will, yes." He watched me with his dark eyes, an unreadable expression on his face.

"Like I don't hate funerals enough."

"Yes, of course," he soothed. "Everyone should realize how difficult this will be for you."

"Yeah, that's—you jerk. I hate you."

"No, you worship the hallowed ground I trod upon, which is what any good wife should—" He ducked, and my left shoe went flying over his head. Fortunately, it missed the window. I couldn't stand the thought of my new pump being torn by flying glass. "My sweet, I was only seeking to give comfort in your time of—"

"Do you *know* how many pairs of shoes I packed?"

"Ah . . . no. Perhaps a change of subject would be prudent. Where is Jessica?"

"Watching BabyJon in her suite. You know, I didn't want her to come, but now I'm awfully glad she did. I don't trust the werewolves with him. There's something weird going on there."

"Mmmmm. What were you up to until the sun set?"

"You wouldn't believe me if I told you."

His eyes narrowed. "No one bothered you, did they?"

"It's not like that, Sinclair." I sighed and sat down across from him. "This is a weird place. I'm not sure I like it. And this whole Council thing is making me nervous. I miss our house. I miss Tina and Laura and Marc. I just want to go home."

"At last," he said, "we are of one mind. Perhaps it will help you to think of the funeral as part of the cost of returning to Minnesota."

"Or perhaps I'll think of it as the werewolf version of Tailhook."

"Either way," he said, glancing at his watch, "we had best get moving. Soonest done, soonest home."

"Dammit. No time for a quickie?"

He smiled at me and shook his head, but I could tell he hated to do it.

"Not even a quickie quickie?"

"Stop that, vile temptress. Now let's be off; people are waiting for us."

Hmph. I'd always thought that whole "jump in and get it over with" thing wasn't always the way to go.

But damned if I was going to cower in a room that wasn't mine, in a house where nobody knew me and nobody cared to. No, I'd go to Antonia's funeral and hold my head up, and if the fuzzy lollipop brigade didn't like it, nuts to them.

Chapter 22

$\mathcal{I}$ knocked, then poked my head into Jessica's room to see how BabyJon was doing. Jessica, resigned, was walking back and forth with him while he alternated crying with spitting up on her shoulder.

"And once again, I can't thank you enough."

"And once again, I need to buy a new shirt." She had to raise her voice to be heard over the baby. "Have fun at the funeral, anyway. Should be a piece of cake, right?"

"It's a joke, that's what it is." I held out my arms and she gladly surrendered him to me. BabyJon hushed at once, except for the occasional hiccup.

"I wouldn't say that around here if I were you,"

she warned, scraping at the fusty left shoulder of her blouse.

"It's the truth, though."

"Come on, Bets. It's hard for them. These guys—from what I've seen, they're a tight bunch. It's probably like losing a niece, or a sister, or—"

"Bullshit. The Pack didn't *like* Antonia, remember? They were glad when she left."

Jess snapped her fingers. "Jeez, you're right! I'd forgotten all about that. It creeped them out that she couldn't change, but could tell the future. They needed her, but they were all sorta scared of her, too."

I nodded. Antonia had gotten abysmally drunk (do you have any idea how much booze a werewolf has to drink before feeling it?) one night a few months back. She'd told us the whole story.

How hardly any of them spoke to her.

How frightened they were of her: Would she withhold her predictions? If she saw something bad in a Pack member's future, would she spill it? Or keep it to herself?

Worst of all, she'd told us how the Pack had been relieved when they'd found out she wasn't coming back. They hadn't missed her at all, or even worried about her.

No. They'd been *relieved*.

And now they expected me to face the music. The whole thing pissed me off.

Jessica was shaking her head. "Glad I'm not in your shoes, Bets. Although they *are* pretty nice," she added, peeking at my pumps.

"They can do whatever they want with me," I muttered. "But if they fuck with my shoes I'm going to kill them all in a variety of horrible ways.

"Gosh." I kissed BabyJon on his sweet head. "I feel safer already."

Chapter 23

Wyndham Manor, I had been told, was not only werewolf HQ and the seat of their power, it was also home to dozens of Pack members. And it had obviously been built to accommodate crowds, because the service was held in a room the size of a warehouse and nobody was crowded. I was guessing, when there wasn't a coffin involved, it was a ballroom.

Michael had spoken briefly, and then a minister (a werewolf Presbyterian minister!) had spoken, and then people started filing past the coffin, no doubt paying their respects.

I had noticed right away that they'd switched

Antonia to a much nicer coffin. It shone like polished jet and was just as black. An enormous spray of white calla lilies nearly covered the entire top. I wonder what they'd done with the old one—the one Derik had destroyed. Then I decided a) it was a morbid thought and b) none of my business.

At least Jessica was missing this. This was actually fine by me—if I knew where she was, I wouldn't worry about her.

BabyJon was snuggled against my shoulder, thumb popped into his mouth, gazing around with bright-eyed interest. I tried to pretend he wasn't drooling on the lapel of my Ann Taylor.

Weirdly, it had been Sinclair's idea for me to bring him. It was the first time Sinclair had suggested we bring BabyJon anywhere, so on top of being sad for Antonia, and scared for us, I was suspicious of my husband's motives.

I didn't move when people started getting up. I had already paid my respects. I had wept over her, called her Pack, and told them the unthinkable, had flown her home. It was more than I'd done for my own father.

"Hello. It's Betsy, right?"

I looked up and almost gasped. One of the most

striking women I had ever seen in my life was standing in front of me, with a pregnant belly out to *here*.

"Uh, yeah." I shifted BabyJon and held out a hand, which she shook briskly. "Betsy Taylor."

"The infamous queen of the dead." But her blue eyes were kind, and she was smiling. Her hair was a rich auburn cloud around her shoulders. "I'm Sara, Derik's wife."

"Undead," I corrected, "and yeah, that's me. Was Antonia a friend of yours? I s'pose she must have been; she and your husband were kind of tight, or so I heard. I'm very sorry about what happened to her."

"Thank you." Sara eased herself into the chair beside me and massaged the small of her back. "But she wasn't my friend. I couldn't stand spending time with her."

I stared. And stared. And stared some more, feeling equal parts admiration and horror. Sara had a pair, that was for sure, to speak ill of the dead in this of all places. But she was telling the truth, which I admired tremendously.

"She *was* kind of a grump," I admitted. "You're, um, not a werewolf. Are you?"

"No, no."

"So Jeannie's not the only human who, ah, runs with the Pack?"

"No indeed. Although I'm not technically human," she said.

"Oh."

"I'm the reincarnation of the sorceress Morgan Le Fay."

Oh. Great. A crazy woman—a crazy *pregnant* woman—was sitting less than two feet away. My, what an interesting week this was turning out to be!

Sara laughed, accurately reading my expression. "Never mind, you don't have to believe it, just like I don't have to convince you. Although I should warn you, if you try to hurt me, the chances are excellent that something awful will happen to you."

"I just met you. Why would I want to hurt you?"

"Nobody knows. Just like no one can predict what you and your husband are up to at any given time. Are you going to finish that?"

I handed her my cherry Coke—yes, now that the actual service was over, they'd broken out the bar drinks. "Predict . . . what the hell are you talking about?"

Sara gestured to the room. I looked, but all I saw were hostile gazes pretty much everywhere I turned.

"You're just making them extremely nervous, that's all."

"What? Me? But that's—"

"You don't have a scent," she interrupted gently. "So they can't tell how you're feeling at any given time. It makes them—all of them—extremely nervous."

Of course! I almost slapped my forehead. I had completely forgotten how much that had weirded Antonia out when she came to live with us. It took her weeks to get used to us for that exact reason.

"Then how come you're on this side of the room, talking to me?"

Sara shrugged. "You don't make me nervous. You're still our guest, despite the circumstances. And you won't be able to hurt me."

Back to that again. "What, are you a superstar pregnant ninja warrior or something?"

"No, no. Nothing like that."

Silence.

"Well? Jeez, you can't make comments like that and then leave me hanging."

"But you won't believe me anyway, so why waste my breath?"

"Try me," I retorted.

She shrugged. "I affect the laws of probability. If someone tries to shoot me, the gun will jam. Or a pinprick aneurysm he had all his life will pick that second to blow. Or he'll miss me and the bullet will ricochet back into his brain."

Sara sighed. "I knew you'd say that."

"I didn't have a chance to say anything, you—" Poor crazy person, I'd been about to say, which wasn't nice, under the circumstances. "So in order for you to—to—uh—"

"Affect the laws of probability."

"Don't you have to do tons of math all the time?"

"Oh, no. My power's completely unconscious. I have no control over it at all. After I won the lottery for the fourth time, I sort of hung it up." She patted her belly. "Besides, there are more important things than buying lottery tickets."

"Yeah, I s'pose."

"And knowing I'll win sort of takes the fun out of it."

"Sure, I can see that." Looney tunes.

"Is this your son?" Sara smiled and held her arms out. BabyJon smiled back and snuggled more firmly into my shoulder.

"It's not you," I hastily assured the crazy pregnant woman. "He pretty much only likes me. He's not my son, though. He's my half brother."

"He's charming," Sara said admiringly. "What beautiful eyes!"

"Thanks." I perked up a little. "He's really a sweet baby. He almost never cries, and he sleeps all day—"

"I would imagine, with a vampire big sister."

"Yeah, we had to do some juggling with everybody's schedule," I admitted.

"But weren't you worried about bringing him here with—with everything that's happened?"

"I haven't been his guardian very long. My husband and I need to get in the habit of thinking like parents, not ravenous, slavering monarchs of the undead."

Sara cracked up, holding her belly and clutching the table so she wouldn't fall over. I perked up even more. At least someone at this funeral didn't blame me for Antonia's sacrifice. I could feel the disapproving stares, but Sara just laughed and laughed.

Finally, she settled down and wiped her watering eyes. "Hormones," she explained. "Sorry."

"Hey, I'm not offended. It's kind of nice to see

someone—" *Lightening up*, I'd been about to say, which would have been seriously uncool.

"So! I've never met a vampire before."

"Well, I've never met a sorceress before." I was trying to remember what I knew about Morgan Le Fay, but history was so not my strong point. I thought she'd been a witch during King Arthur's time. She was one of the bad guys, I was pretty sure. Well, I could always ask Sinclair.

"We can't say that any longer, can we?" Sara was asking.

"Not hardly." I glanced over her shoulder and saw Derik stomping toward us, his normally smiling countenance twisted into a scowl. "Uh-oh. Pissed off hubby at six o'clock."

Sara sighed. "It's been awful for him; I'm sure you can relate. He doesn't mean to act like you shoved Antonia into a hail of bullets. But it's hard. You know?"

I did know. Derik was playing Pin the Blame on the Vampire as an alternative to facing up to the fact that the only reason Antonia left was because most of the Pack disliked her, or were scared of her. I understood, even though I didn't like it one bit. Where was all this concern when she decided to leave town and never come back?

And here he was, looming over our table. "I'd like you to step away from my wife, please," he managed through gritted teeth. "I don't want—aaaggghhh!"

At first I thought he had slipped. Then I realized he'd seen BabyJon and jerked backward so hard, and so fast, that he lost his balance.

"*That* again! Get that baby away from my wife!"

You know those moments in parties where you have to talk loud to be heard, only you do it the one time everyone's quiet? So they all hear exactly what you're shouting?

Yeah. It was like that.

Chapter 24

Dude,

It wasn't long before Laura had a chance to implement Operation Distract. Yes, another band of devil worshippers showed up. But this time she (we, actually) was ready for them.

"Oh most gracious and dread lady," their leader was proclaiming, kneeling before her. His fellow lemmings followed suit, which meant there were sixteen religious extremists in one of our parlors. "We but live to serve you in any capacity you require. Only point us to your enemies and we shall wreak vengeance in your name. In your father's name, Lucifer Morningstar."

That was kind of interesting, because we knew Laura's mother had been possessed by the devil. And the devil always appeared to Laura (you can imagine her mood after one of those fun-filled visits) as a woman.

I imagine the Prince/Princess of Lies can appear as anything he/she wants.

"We are yours to command!" he shouted at Laura's feet, since they were all cowering before her on their knees. None of them could see the way she shook her head in disgust, rolling her eyes. "Oh most dread sovereign, your coming was foretold and it has come at last!"

"Yes, yes," she replied impatiently. "That's fine. Now. You. All of you."

All the heads jerked up at once. It was like watching otters pop their heads out of the water at the zoo.

"I bid ye go forth. All of you find the soup kitchen on Lake and Fourth, in Minneapolis. Volunteer for at least fifty hours a week."

The leader's sad basset hound face seemed to sag even further. "But—but we wish to—"

"Are you questioning me?" Laura thundered in a pretty good imitation of an angry demigod wearing

a pink sweater. "You dare question how I test your loyalty?"

Practically elbowing each other out of the way, they all denied questioning anything.

"So begone from here, and do my unholy bidding at Sister Sue's Soup Kitchen. I will know when you are ready."

They all galloped out, several of them getting wedged in the doorway in their eagerness to obey Laura's completely unevil command.

They were no sooner out the front door than Laura threw herself into my arms hard enough to rock me back on my heels. "It worked! Oh, Marc, I can't thank you enough, what a wonderful idea you had!"

"Fifty hours a week should keep them out of trouble," I agreed, patting her back.

"Oh, I don't know why I didn't think of this before!"

Well, honey, you pretty much tense up and close off whenever anything connecting you with your mother gets shoved in your face. When you're that angry, or that upset, or that sad, it's impossible to think logically.

(Dude, I prudently kept that to myself.)

"I don't know how I kept a straight face," Laura gasped. "I looked at you and I almost lost it right in front of that band of dimwitted sheep."

In all modesty, I had to admit my idea stank with the reek of genius. Put them to work for you, I'd said. Make them volunteer at homeless shelters, at soup kitchens, at church fund-raisers. That way they're happy—they think they're being tested—and you're happy because not only are they out of your hair, they're spending virtually all their free time helping the greater good.

I'd saved the best for last: ordering devil worshippers to commit good deeds was a terrific way to defy her mother. If I had needed a deal closer, that was it.

"Marc, if there's ever anything I can do for you, you have to come see me or call."

"Are you kidding? You just gave me ten minutes of free entertainment. You're square with the house, honey."

Laura turned away for a moment, suddenly lost in thought. "Maybe I've been looking at this the wrong way. If they'll do anything I say—if they'll do things for me they would do for no one else—I wonder what else I can make them do?"

"Hey, one way to find out," I said, having absolutely no idea that I was inadvertently, and with the best of intentions, driving Laura to a break with her conscience and her sanity.

I take full responsibility for the following events, which I will narrate as quickly and carefully as I can.

Chapter 25

erik! Apologize this minute," Sara practically hissed. "I know you're upset, but this is ridiculous. He's just a baby."

"I don't know what the hell that thing is," Derik retorted, "but it's not a baby."

"You're acting like you've seen a ghoul, or something," Jeannie said.

"What baby?"

Jeannie turned to her husband. "What baby? The one she got off the plane with, what are you talking about, what baby?"

Oh, great, here were Michael and Jeannie Wyndham, with Sinclair hot on their heels.

"Everybody just calm down," I began, but Derik drowned me out.

He pointed. "That baby."

Michael frowned. "But you don't have a baby."

Jeannie stared. "What's wrong with you?" She nodded toward Derik. "Him, I get. He's just playing the blame game. But you—"

I was flabbergasted. I'd suspected last night he hadn't noticed BabyJon, but not noticing or commenting was one thing. Michael didn't appear to *see* my brother at all.

"Well, he's not mine," I said, trying to recover from my surprise. "I mean, he is now. He's my brother."

Michael was staring at BabyJon with his flat, yellow gaze. "Where did he come from?"

"Uh, Michael." I coughed. "Um, he came with us. On the plane, like Jeannie said. He was in the limo with us last night. And in your office."

"Oh, well, that's fine then."

"I wouldn't call that exactly fine," Jeannie began, but Michael had already turned away, gently touching Jeannie's elbow.

"Hon, would you tell the kitchen they need to send up more—"

"Wait."

Sinclair might not have been a Pack member, but he had no trouble seizing control of a moment . . . Everybody stopped and looked at him.

"Michael," Sinclair asked quietly, almost gently, "where is the baby?"

Michael frowned and cocked his head, as if listening to a voice from another room. "What baby?"

"That's it," Jeannie said firmly. "I'm taking you to a doctor. Right now."

"I'm not sure it's something a doctor can fix," I said, mentally reeling. I mean, I really needed a minute here.

As soon as Michael had turned his back, he'd forgotten—again—about BabyJon. Derik wouldn't go anywhere near the kid. And the other werewolves seemed to be picking up on Derik's extreme stress. Only Sara seemed unperturbed.

"Perhaps it's time to go," Sinclair murmured, his fingers clutching the back of my chair.

Perhaps it was time to call the local mental hospital with some new admits. "Uh, okay," I said, slowly getting to my feet. BabyJon, unmoved by recent events, yawned against my neck. "Well, thanks for the—uh—snacks. I guess we'll—"

"We're not going to actually let them get *away* with this, are we?" A petite, dark-haired woman with a severe buzz cut was standing on the fringe of our small group. She was dressed in black jeans and a black button-down shirt, and it took me a minute to place her.

It was Cain—one of the werewolves who'd come to the mansion looking for Antonia earlier in the week.

"She gets Antonia killed, then brings some sort of ensorcelled infant—if that's what it really is—and we're just going to let her walk?"

"Cain."

"Well, *are* we?" she cried, turning to face the man who towered over her. He, too, was dark and whip-thin. He, too, looked weirded out but, even more than that, he seemed almost embarrassed. For her or for me, I had no idea. But I wasn't going to bet the farm it was me.

"That's for the Council to decide," the quiet, dark-haired man said. "Not us. And not here."

"But she got Antonia killed! And she doesn't even seem to care!"

And that was just about enough. "I didn't get Antonia killed," I said, and I could practically feel ears pricking up all over the room. "You did."

Sinclair pinched the bridge of his nose and shook his head.

"And then she—*what*?" Cain's jaw sagged and she turned to fully face me. "What did you say to me?"

"What's wrong? Should I get a megaphone? Do you not understand English?" Smiling, I beckoned her closer and, when she bent to hear, I said loudly, "I didn't get Antonia killed. You did."

Cain jerked away and rubbed her ear. A few more werewolves sidled over. Sinclair was still shaking his head and looking like the before picture of a sinus headache commercial.

"I am so sick of this bullshit," I said, knowing my voice was carrying, knowing *everyone* in the room could hear me, and not much caring. "I guess it hasn't occurred to any of you to ask yourselves what the hell Antonia was doing living with vampires in the first place. Oh, hell no! After all, it's much more convenient to blame us than face the fact that she couldn't get out of *here* fast enough."

"And now," Sinclair sighed, "we fight."

"Here," I said, thrusting BabyJon toward Sara, who scooped him up and backed off a couple of steps. BabyJon let out a pissed-off yowl, ignoring Sara's attempts to soothe him.

"You can't pass the buck that easily," Cain retorted. "You were the leader; she was your responsibility."

"She was a grown woman, you nitwit! You're making it sound like she was my kindergarten student."

"You're still passing the buck," someone else said, a werewolf I hadn't met.

"And *you're* all conveniently overlooking the fact that not only did you practically drive her to my front door, I didn't see *any* of you assholes ever come to visit."

"She was her own person," that same werewolf said.

"Well, which is it, dipshit? Either she was a grown woman who could take care of herself, or she needed me to shelter and protect her. You can't have it both ways."

"We're getting a bit far afield," Sinclair began, but I bulldozed right over him.

"She didn't get a single phone call the entire time she lived with us. The only time anyone bothered to show up was after she missed her weekly military check-in, whatever it was. When your info pipeline into the vampires suddenly got cut off, *then* you showed up."

A furious gabble of voices rose, and rose, and I had to shout to be heard over the din. "Not to mention, *not to mention*, you guys clearly didn't want much to do with her while she was alive. So all this postmortem concern is a pile of crap. You guys look stupid trying to come off all morally outraged when it was *your* fault she was living in my house in the first place."

The babble of voices got louder, but I was able to pick out one comment from the din: "The bottom line is that she died in your service, so it's your responsibility."

"If they're even telling the truth about how she died," someone else said. "How can we ever know? She and her mate don't have a scent. They can make up any story they like and we'd never know the difference."

"Oh, really? Okay. Here's a story, fuck-o. Once upon a time, there was a werewolf who could predict the future who lived on Cape Cod. And all her supposed friends and family went out of their way to avoid her because she wasn't exactly Miss Congeniality." I ought to know; I used to be one. "And one day she moved away and never came back, and nobody in her Pack gave a rat's ass. The end."

More babbling. The din rose and rose. Shouts. Threats. Michael trying to get everyone to calm down. Sinclair rubbing the bridge of his nose. Sara looking like an increasingly nervous tennis match observer. BabyJon crying.

It was stupid, really. Stupid to forget how fast they were. Stupid to pick a fight in a room full of werewolves. I heard the crash of a chair splintering, and turned just in time to get stabbed in the heart with a chair leg.

That was pretty much when the lights went out.

Chapter 26

Dude,

I swear my intentions were good. But I vastly overestimated Laura's state of mind and underestimated the rapidity with which things could deteriorate. And when Tina started having trouble sending and receiving e-mails, I honestly didn't make the connection until it was too late.

But I'm getting ahead of myself.

More Satanists showed up and, instead of hiding from them or being embarrassed by them, Laura started briskly giving them orders. She spent a lot of time on the web finding charitable organizations where she could send the devil worshippers, and soon there were Satanists all over the metro area, cheerfully raising money for the homeless or participating in Meals on Wheels.

I admit, dude, I was proud of myself. I didn't go into medicine for the money, obviously, so helping people always put me in a good mood. And Laura, for all her advantages, needed me as much as any patient. It's just too damn bad I was too busy patting myself on the back to notice what was really going on.

Tina came and went, always on her own schedule, and I knew better than to ask her what she was up to. Mostly because it was none of my business, but also because she was as closed-mouthed about her work as I was about mine.

There had been a bad crack-up on I-35—no fatalities, thank God—so I didn't get home until about 2:30 A.M. I headed straight for the kitchen (I had finally gone grocery shopping, so there was actual food in the fridge), where I found Tina sitting at the counter with her laptop, muttering to herself.

"Hey."

"Good morning," she said, not looking up.

"Everything okay?"

"Mmmm." Then, thoughtfully, "You had a busy night, I see."

Ah. Right. I had found it prudent to change out of my scrubs the moment I got home—or, even better, before I left the hospital. It didn't matter if the blood on me was ten minutes old or ten hours. They could always smell it.

"Car crash."

"Mmmm."

I set about making myself a tuna sandwich while Tina pecked away at her laptop. She seemed a little off—annoyed, maybe, or distracted.

"Everything okay?"

"Hmmm?" She looked around as if noticing me for the first time. "Oh. Yes, everything's fine. I'm getting a poor wireless signal. My e-mails to His Majesty keep bouncing."

"So call."

"I have."

"Oh. You don't think anything's wrong, do you?"

"I'm sure they're fine."

I believed her. But I also knew what was bugging her. Tina lived for Betsy and Sinclair, the way most *people lived for racing cars or marathons. When she couldn't keep in touch, she got antsy. Not unlike a drug addict going through withdrawal, to be perfectly blunt.*

"Betsy answered my e-mail," I volunteered. It was a typical Betsy missive: bitchy and shrill. She really hated e-mail acronyms. The woman should really catch up to this century's lingo. "I'm sure she's already won over the werewolves and they're somewhere partying like it's 1999."

Tina slapped the laptop closed and smiled at me. "I'm sure you're right. Now, if you'll excuse me, I must go out."

To hunt. And feed. She was too polite to say so, of course. But I sure as hell wasn't going to stand in her way. A grumpy vampire is a homicidal vampire. Hungry ones were even worse.

"Heck," I called after her, "they've probably declared it National Betsy Day out on Cape Cod. You know she can win over just about anybody."

Yes, dude, I know. In retrospect that was beyond ignorant. But how was I supposed to know they were going to kill her?

Chapter 27

$\mathcal{I}$ opened my eyes and saw a ring of tense faces above me. The first few times this had happened to me I'd been badly startled, but now I was getting used to being killed and then brought back to life.

"Ow," I commented, sitting up. There was a sizeable hole in my blouse and suit jacket. Not to mention an unconscious werewolf three feet away. And BabyJon was still howling. "You'd better give him to me."

Wide-eyed, Sara knelt beside me and obliged. BabyJon hushed at once, giving me a chance to take a good look around.

"Oh, man," I said, eyeing the werewolf who, I

assumed, had driven a chair leg into my heart. "Sinclair, what did you do to him?"

"I only hit him once," my husband replied in that faux-casual tone that didn't fool me one bit.

"Where'd everybody go?"

Aside from Sara, Sinclair, Jeannie, Michael, Baby-Jon, and Derik, the room was empty. Oh, and let's not forget the werewolf who killed me.

"Michael cleared the room after you were attacked. Ah—it's none of my business," Sara continued, "but why aren't you a pile of dust?"

"It's a queen of the undead thing," I said, trying to get my feet under me so I could stand. Sinclair gripped one of my arms, Michael the other, and they hauled me up. I stared down at my ruined suit and sighed.

"I must apologize on the Pack's behalf," Michael said stiffly. He appeared calm, but I had the distinct impression he was mortified.

And Jeannie was *pissed*. "There was no excuse for that. At all." She turned to Sinclair. "You should have torn his damned head off."

"Maybe next time," my husband replied.

"Again, I apologize." Michael nodded at the still-snoring werewolf. "He will be dealt with; you have my word."

"No, don't."

"Sorry, what?"

"Just forget it."

"Elizabeth," my husband began warningly.

"Let's not make things any worse than they already are. Look! No harm, no foul. I'm fine. He can buy me a new suit and we'll call it even."

"Unacceptable," Sinclair said flatly and, wonder of wonders, Michael was nodding in agreement. Finally, they had a goal in common: ignoring my express wishes.

But for a change I had the chance to be the better man—so to speak—and moved to take advantage of it. Maybe I was beginning to think more politically in my old age. "I mean it, you guys. Let it go. It was a bad situation for all of us. It's not like I didn't provoke him. Come on, let's forget about it and move on. This Council thing—when are we supposed to talk to them?"

"Tomorrow," Michael said, giving me a look I'd never seen on his face before. Grudging admiration? Disbelief in my sanity? Maybe he just had to use the bathroom. "Midnight."

Ah, yes. Midnight. Not too big of a cliché. But I kept that to myself—I'd shot my mouth off enough for one night.

"So, we'll be there. But let's call it a night for now. I don't know about you guys, but I've had about all the excitement I can take for one day. Night. Whatever."

Sara laughed; she was the only one who did. But at least the others seemed to tacitly agree, because they fell back and let Sinclair, BabyJon, and me get back to our suite.

"Are you okay?" I muttered out of the side of my mouth, patting BabyJon on the rump. Hoo! The boy needed a diaper change in the worst way.

"I am deeply, deeply regretting not putting my fist through your attacker's skull," Sinclair replied neutrally.

"Don't worry. There's always tomorrow."

Sinclair snorted, but seemed to lighten up. That was a good, good thing. I'm sure the werewolves were all badass and everything, but none of them had a thing on my husband, who wasn't only a) the king of the vampires and b) old and wily, but c) wouldn't tolerate people messing with me.

If they hadn't learned that after tonight, there was no hope for them, and no hope for reconciliation. And then what?

War, maybe. A vampire/werewolf war.

Swell.

Chapter 28

My king,

Things here are as well as can be expected. I have reviewed the quarterly report from your holdings in Los Angeles and it seems the new security system for the company's web server is doing the job.

Laura seems to be entertaining quite a bit in your absence; it seems there are always strangers in the house. Neither Marc nor Laura has said anything to me about them, so I am respecting their privacy and assuming they are trying to fill the void left by the absence of you and the queen.

I trust this finds you and Her Majesty well. If you require anything of me, do not hesitate to contact me at once. In the meantime, I have FedExed copies of the contracts for your most recently acquired properties. Please review them at your leisure, sign them if they are satisfactory, and return them to me. I will then take the next step.
My love and fealty to you both.
—Tina

"See?" I whined. "Why can't I get e-mails like that? Not only is it clear and understandable, it's in English!"

"My love, what in the world are you talking about?"

"Look!" I stabbed a finger at the printout of Marc's latest rambling.

hey, grrrrl, miss you bad. things out here are BTW, but I've got a handle on it. Laura says howdy and wants you to GBH ASAP. tell your magically delicious hubby to answer tina's e-mails; the grrl is FRO! later, marc.

"I have no idea what he's talking about," I muttered. "This might as well be in French."

"What is a FRO?" Sinclair asked, studying the printout.

"My point! How should I know? When I send an e-mail, I actually spell words out. *And* use punctuation."

"Light of my life, while I enjoy tirelessly listening to your never-ending litany of complaints, I believe we have slightly more pressing matters to discuss. For example, your attempted murder. And our appearance before the Council."

"Yeah, yeah. But we're getting back to this e-mail thing."

We'd been back in our suite for about twenty minutes. The first thing Sinclair did was strip me out of my ruined suit and blouse and examine me from head to toe. It was a waste of time—I was fine. But sometimes there was no talking to the stubborn cuss I had married.

"So, dish." I had put BabyJon down for a midnight nap and was lying on our bed, covertly feeling my chest now and again. Nope, no gaping holes. "What happened after I got stabbed?"

"Oh, the usual. Pandemonium. Violence. Threats. More violence."

"You suck at narratives."

He bowed his head modestly. I knew I was wasting my breath (so to speak). Sinclair wasn't about to confess that he'd been scared out of his mind yet again. He liked to play it cool, even with me.

"Logically, your attempted murder can only help us."

"Gee, thanks. So glad to be of service." I sat up and swung my right leg out to kick him in the shin, which he neatly avoided.

"Elizabeth, you know exactly what I mean."

"Michael's humiliated and mortified, which the Council will pick up on? Like that?"

"Yes. Like that."

"They must have been pretty surprised when I got up off the floor."

He grinned. "Yes, indeed. Once I was able to remove the chair leg from your sternum, you woke up almost instantly—and healed as quickly."

"Glad to be of help. That Sara girl was nice. She was about the only one who was nice."

He shrugged and eased out of his jacket. "Give

them time. Your warped charm will eventually win them over."

"Hypocrites. Is it just me, or did Antonia never get a call or a visit from these guys the whole time she was living with us?"

"It is not just you. But take comfort in the fact that in the last year of her life Antonia found love and happiness with us. Something she apparently could not get out here."

That was sad. These yo-yos were supposed to be her family. But nobody had much cared until she was killed. Hell, they hadn't even known she was in a committed relationship with another vampire—Garrett, who had killed himself about four seconds after he'd realized the love of his life was dead.

It was all too awful to contemplate and for a moment I envied Jessica, lying in a dark bedroom and sleeping through this entire rotten mess.

But that was no way to be; it certainly didn't solve anything. We had to move forward—even if it meant leaving some people behind.

Chapter 29

Dude,

It's really hard to write this. I'm embarrassed and mad at myself. But I'd better get it off my chest, so listen up.

I can pinpoint the exact moment I realized the shit was hitting the fan. It was the next morning, long after Tina had retired for the day. I was minding my own business, wolfing down a bowl of Special K and reading the latest John Sandford novel, when Laura bopped in.

She seemed more cheerful than usual, which was nice, because she'd been awfully stressed since Betsy and Sinclair left. And she looked even prettier than usual—and Laura was a beautiful girl—with her buttercup yellow sweater and faded jeans, her blond hair pulled back in its perpetual ponytail, big eyes bright and sparkling.

"Morning!" she chirped, sitting across from me. "Did I get any calls?"

"Uh, no. Are you expecting one?"

"Sure. I had this great idea and I have you to thank for it. I'll hopefully find out today if it worked."

Dude, I should have followed up right then. But I didn't. I figured she was involved with some church thing, or was working on a project for school. I'm an ER resident, not a shrink. How was I supposed to know she'd lost her mind?

Yeah, I know. It's all just a bunch of crap justification now. I should have been paying closer attention, and I wasn't. That's the long and short of it.

"It's going to solve a lot of problems," Laura continued, and I admit I was barely listening to her. "I've just been so worried about Betsy ever since she almost died (again) when Antonia got shot."

"Betsy's always almost dying again." I was a little more sanguine about the vampire queen's resilience; I had seen many, many strange things since Betsy

stopped me from killing myself a couple years back.
"She's like our own personal Kenny."

"Kenny?"

"From South Park. Pop culture reference; sorry." Laura tended to stick to network news and the Food Network. A single episode of South Park would horrify and disgust her. Sometimes the show horrified me, too, but I was still addicted to it. Nobody's perfect.

"Where's Tina?"

"Conked out in her room—you know how it is with her. She won't be going anywhere until the sun's down."

"I have something for her," Laura said vaguely. "And some people want to see her."

"Great." I yawned. New vampires were always stopping by the mansion to pay their respects. "Thank God it's my day off. I need a break from sick people."

Laura giggled. "That's an odd thing for a doctor to say."

"Honey, all doctors say it. Just not around patients."

"I'm sure that's—"

The phone rang and Laura leaped to her feet, practically sprinting to get it before it rang again. I rolled my eyes; probably some church wanted her to run a fund-raiser or some such thing. Or maybe PBS was running another pledge drive.

"Yes? Hello?" She paused, listening. "Okay, great! That's just great . . . uh-huh . . . really? Oh, you didn't!" She laughed, then paused again. "Uh-huh . . . you are? Terrific. Then I'll see you in a bit. Thanks very much." She hung up.

"Good news?" I yawned.

"The best news. Okay, well, I've got to go. See you."

"Bye," I said vaguely, and I was back into my book before she got to the front door.

So, so careless. Not to mention stupid. It's all fine and good to say now "How was I supposed to know?" except I had seen the effect the devil worshippers had on Laura. I should have been suspicious of her 180, instead of focusing on my own problems.

But I wasn't.

And, though I didn't know it, it was already too late.

Chapter 30

ou mean someone killed you again? And I missed it?" Jessica groaned and covered her face. "Damn! I was washing puke from my clothes while you were getting murdered . . . Dammit!"

"You didn't miss much," I soothed. "Just me picking a fight with a bunch of werewolves, getting stabbed, Sinclair kicking the crap out of my stabber, me waking up, and then everybody taking off."

"Oh, sure. Sounds like a real snoozefest. So what happens next?"

"We're supposed to meet the Council tonight."

"Why?"

I shrugged. I was still a little vague on that myself.

Jessica and I were having a late-afternoon drink in the sitting room of my suite. Because it was barely five o'clock, BabyJon was still asleep, and so was Sinclair.

I had my own thoughts about that, but kept them to myself. See, Sinclair could move around during the day, he just couldn't go outside. The fact that he was choosing to stay under told me he was storing up his strength for whatever ordeal lay ahead. And, typical of Sinclair, he wasn't telling me any of the things he was worrying about.

"So, what?" Jess was saying, blowing on her hot chocolate. "You tell them what happened, and they do what?"

"I have no idea."

"You shouldn't even be talking to them."

"What?"

Jessica sipped. Blew. Sipped again. "You did what you had to do. Just like Antonia. So why should you have to explain yourself to a bunch of strangers who apparently never gave that poor girl a thought once she blew town?"

"It's why we came out here," I said. "We knew we'd have to face the music one way or another."

"I don't like it. I never liked it. You shouldn't take the defensive."

I shrugged. "Let's see how it plays out. A few hundred people noticed last night that I'm pretty tough to kill. And—holy crap, I forgot to tell you about what happened with the baby!"

I summed it up for Jess, who was amazed. "Come on. Michael really forgot you brought a *baby* out here?"

"He totally, completely did."

"Weird."

"Tell me! And Derik freaked out again."

"Here all this time we thought werewolves were vulnerable to silver bullets, when it's dirty diapers that they fear."

I snorted with laughter, nearly spilling my own cup of cocoa. "Oh, and I met this really nice woman—"

"Let me guess: not a werewolf."

"No, but she's married to one. She was really nice, for a crazy lady."

"That's what they said about Lorena Bobbitt."

I shook my head at her. Jess could always cheer me up. She could always put things in perspective for me. I hadn't wanted her to come on this trip, but now I was glad she had.

"This whole thing has me thinking."

"I'll call the newspapers," she replied. "Maybe even take a picture of you thinking and post it on a website somewhere. Dammit again! My phone's on the plane with Cooper."

"I'm sure they have phones here if you need to make a call."

"Not this time. You're the one I always call—God knows why—and you're just across the hallway. By the way, these walls aren't soundproofed. You think you can keep it down while you're making the beast with two backs?"

"Knock it off, you bitch. I've been thinking that Michael and I are very different kinds of leaders."

"Well, you don't like to lead anybody. You've been saying since day one that vampires should police themselves."

"Right. But see, Michael knows how many werewolves are in the Pack. He knows where they live and who they are. But me, not so much. I have *no* idea how many vampires are running around. And even if I did, I'd have no idea how to get in touch with them. Say, God forbid, there's a war between vamps and weres. We'd be fucked, because the werewolves are a species. They're born werewolves and they know who they are and where they're going. But vampires are made. *Violently* made. So why should they feel any loyalty to other vampires? I sure don't.

I mean, I'm loyal to Tina and Sinclair, but they're family. None of the other vamps are."

"So there you are."

"What?"

"Now you know what you've got to do."

"Terrific. Care to share with the rest of the class?"

"Prevent a war. At all costs, prevent a war. Because it sounds to me like you'd lose, and lose big." For once, Jessica wasn't teasing. She looked very sober and she was gripping her cup so hard her hands shook. "You can't afford it, Betsy. None of us can."

"They don't know I've got the devil's daughter on my side."

"You really want to put Laura through that? That girl's already walking a fine line between too good and really nuts."

"You're right. It'd be a rotten thing to do." But I made a mental note to keep it in mind. If worse came to worst, we'd fight. And if worse came to terrible, I had the devil's daughter as my secret weapon.

I guess that's what being a leader meant. Using people for your own ends, even if you knew it was a bad idea.

Great.

Chapter 31

Jess had gone back to her room to get dressed for the Council, and Sinclair was working away at his laptop, when I decided to get some fresh air. I was taking a stroll down the beach when I saw the ghost. She waved at me tentatively, and I waved back.

This had been one of the hardest things for me to get used to, almost as difficult to accept as the fact that I had to drink blood to survive. Like the kid from *The Sixth Sense*, I saw dead people. Also like that kid, they tended to scare the crap out of me. Given how scared I was of ghosts and zombies, I wasn't unaware of the irony that I was now one of the monsters. Didn't like it, but understood the grisly joke life (or death) had played on me.

Unfortunately, ignoring the ghosts just made it worse . . . When they saw I wasn't hopping to obey their edicts from beyond the grave, they got more aggressive. Hung around all the time. Popped out of nowhere when you were, say, having sex with your husband.

My favorite ghost—Cathie, victim of the serial killer Laura had killed—and my least favorite—the Ant—both came and went without warning. In fact, I hadn't seen Cathie in almost a year. This bummed me out a bit, and when I thought of her I always hoped she'd gone on to better things.

As for the Ant, I was just grateful she'd disappeared and hadn't come back. Yet.

So, though I didn't much want to, I walked up to the ghost and said howdy.

"Excuse me," she said politely, interrupting me mid introduction. "But how in the world can you see me?"

"Vampire."

"But there are no vampires. And it's still light out."

"There are, and it is, but it's a long story, so why don't you just tell me why you're haunting the beach so we can get on with our lives? Or deaths. Whatever."

The ghost, a pale brunette with her hair pulled back in a bun, appeared to think that over for a bit. She was wearing clothes that were clearly from the 1960s, poor thing (of all the decades to be trapped in, fashionwise!), and was wearing cat's-eye glasses. We were far enough down the beach that my feet were getting wet as the waves slopped over them, but they just went right through the ghost's shoes without doing any damage. Luckily, I was wearing last year's sandals.

"Would you mind giving a message to my son?"

"If I can find him, sure."

"Would you please tell him I would prefer he not name his unborn child after me?"

"Seriously? That's it? That's why your spirit can't rest?"

"My name is Theodocia," she said.

"Oh." The horror! "Jeez. I'm really sorry. I'll be glad to pass that on for you."

"Thank you kindly."

Chapter 32

Dude,

The shit officially hit the fan later that night. I was online, chatting with an old boyfriend from Oregon, when I heard a racket downstairs. I logged off and went to see what the problem was.

The problem was Laura, surrounded by people so completely deferential to her that I knew at once we had more devil worshippers on our hands.

"You did it?" Laura asked. "You actually did it?"

"It was easy, dread mistress! Two of us acted as bait, and we were able to surround it and kill it with no trouble at all."

"Kill what?" I asked, halfway down the stairs.

Laura looked up at me and the smile dropped off her face. "Nothing, Marc. We're sorry to disturb you."

"What's going on?"

"The Beloved of Samael has told you: nothing. Now away with you, or you'll find out exactly what we killed," one of the half dozen around her snapped.

Laura rested her hand on his shoulder. "Don't speak to him like that," she said quietly. "He's my sister's friend."

And yours, honey.

The man, taller than Laura by almost a foot, and at least thirty pounds heavier, instantly acquiesced, and even bowed his head in compliance. Good dog, nice dog, woof-woof-woof.

"Laura, what the hell is going on?"

"Come into the kitchen and I'll explain." She turned to the group. "You all know what to do. Come find me tomorrow and let me know how it went."

There was a chorus of "Yes, dread mistress!" and "At once, my lady!" and then they all galloped toward the foyer leading to the front door.

I followed Laura to the kitchen, where she turned and gave me a smile that was much too bright.

"I'm helping Betsy," she confided.

"Uh-huh. Helping her how?"

"Well." Laura helped herself to a glass of milk, guzzled half of it, then continued. "You know I've been worried about her ever since that awful, awful thing with Antonia."

"Yeah," I said, still mystified.

"I promised myself that if I could do anything to keep her from harm, I would. Anything in my power. Because she's my only sister, and she can't help being a sinner. None of us can!"

Oh, cripes, I hated when she went on these pseudoreligious original sin rants. But I kept a pleasantly neutral expression on my face. "And?"

"Okay. So I've been trying to figure out just what I can do. And her and Sinclair going to the Cape is the perfect time, right?"

"Why?"

"Because she listens to him too much," she said impatiently. "I warned her not to marry him, but she didn't listen. But with him gone, I only had Tina to worry about."

The hairs on the back of my neck were trying to

stand up. Fortunately, thanks to years of practice as an MD, I was able to keep my expression neutral. "Where is Tina, Laura?"

She waved that away. "Never mind. The important thing, the most wonderful thing, is that the sinners who keep finding me—they're helping me save Betsy! I never would have thought of it if it hadn't been for you, Marc."

Oh, shit. "Maybe you'd better not give me the credit until you tell me exactly what it is you and the Satan Brigade have been up to."

"Killing vampires!" Laura said brightly, oblivious of her milk moustache.

"Killing vampires."

"Sure. They keep coming here to pay tribute, and we've managed to send almost a half dozen of them straight to my mother. Straight to hell," she added, unable to keep the dark satisfaction out of her voice.

"Oh my God," I said, appalled. "You didn't. Tell me you didn't."

"Of course I did. We did. You were so right, Marc. Put the devil worshippers to work doing good. And I have!"

I felt my stomach drop into my feet. I couldn't even begin to imagine how much trouble this was *going to be . . . for Betsy, for Sinclair, for Laura, for me. And even if there were no consequences to killing vampires (ha!), Laura had clearly lost it.*

Her affect was all wrong. She was smiling, laughing, happy. But her eyes had a flat shine that I didn't like, and she'd gone out of her way to keep this from me until I forced the issue.

Was I a sinner, too?

Expendable?

Sure I was. The fundamentally religious were not exactly known for their tolerance of homosexuality. Quite the opposite. I imagined it would only be a matter of time before Laura decided she needed to "save" Betsy from me.

Who were the vampires? What had they wanted? And what was going to happen when people realized the queen's sister was killing them?

Civil war?

Worse?

"Where's Tina?" I asked, struggling to keep my voice calm and even.

"You don't need to worry about that, Marc."

"But I am, Laura. She lives here, too. She's Betsy's friend, just like I am."

"Oh, no!" Laura looked shocked at the very

idea. "She's nothing like you, Marc. And you have to understand, I couldn't start helping Betsy until I got her out of the way."

Oh my God. *She'd killed her.* Tina was a pile of dust somewhere.

And it was all my fault.

I pulled out my cell phone, but Laura just shook her head and smiled at me. "I canceled everyone's cell service—you're all on the same plan."

That would explain the fact that instead of a cell phone, I was holding a useless piece of metal and plastic.

"Oh, Laura," I said, and dropped my head into my hands.

Chapter 33

Betsy!

OMG you've got to get back ASAP because TSIATHTF!!!! Grab the gang and CBRA! Right now!

"You see what I mean?" I bitched, showing Jessica Marc's latest acronym-strewn e-mail. "How am I supposed to make heads or tails out of this? He could be asking me to schedule a massage for all I know."

Jessica shrugged. "Can't help you with that one. Gives me a headache just to look at it. Besides, don't you have more important things to worry about?"

"Damn straight. I had to listen to Sinclair's shrill bitching when he couldn't make his cell phone work. Big baby—you'd think the thing was permanently attached to his head. I suggested he call from the mansion, but his stubborn paranoia kicked in and he refused. He's sure the phones are all tapped. The thing of it is, he's probably right. Did you know the full moon is tomorrow?"

"Sure."

"Can you—wait. You did?"

Jessica gave me a look. "I checked before we boarded the plane. Since we were heading into the belly of the beast, so to speak."

"Yeah, well, I've had a few too many things on my mind lately to look up things like moon phases."

"Yes, of course, for example: Is there a shoe sale at Macy's today?"

"I hate you."

Jessica shook her head and smiled at me. "Nice try, but I know I'm your hero."

"Hero," I began, "isn't exactly the word I'd—"

Sinclair stepped into the small sitting area before we could really get going, splendidly dressed in a dark suit and his Kenneth Coles.

"You clean up good," Jessica commented, and he bowed his head in acknowledgment.

"Are you all right, hon? You look a little distracted. Is your phone working now?"

"No, they're claiming someone canceled our service and it will be a few hours before the cells work. And Tina hasn't responded to my e-mails."

The man did pick the oddest things to fret about. "It's probably a bad signal or something. Besides, don't you think we've got slightly more pressing things to worry about?"

"No doubt, my love. I suggest we try to reconcile with the Council tonight so as not to face several hundred angry werewolves tomorrow evening."

"Say it twice," I said, inwardly groaning. Man oh man, the hits just kept on coming. I actually envied Marc, back in St. Paul with nothing more pressing to worry about than whether or not he had time to hit Cub Foods before his shift started.

Lucky bastard.

Chapter 34

We were back in the ballroom, except it had been set up almost like a courtroom. A long table was at the front of the room, and hundreds of chairs were scattered about.

Because we weren't sure just what everyone's problem with BabyJon was, I had prevailed upon Jessica to watch him for me during the whole Council thing.

She'd protested—boy, had she protested, my ears were still ringing—but finally agreed. Good thing, too, because after last night I didn't trust anyone out here to watch him, except maybe for Sara. And I didn't like asking favors from someone I'd just met.

I had dressed up for the occasion, as Sinclair had, in a knee-length black dress with a simple strand of pearls my mom had given me for my sweet sixteen. Manolo pumps in deep purple—they went with almost everything, especially black—completed the picture of a sophisticated vampire queen (ha!).

"Perhaps we should discuss a plan in case things do not go our way this evening," Sinclair murmured, his hand on the small of my back as we walked in.

"Run like hell?" I suggested, and he grinned, whip-quick, there and gone almost before I could register the expression.

Michael came forward to greet us, Jeannie right beside him as usual. "Hello, Betsy. Hello, Eric. Thank you for coming."

Sure, pal. Like we had a choice.

"I'll introduce you to the Council, and they'll ask you some questions about what happened the night Antonia was killed."

"As you like," Sinclair said politely.

"Good luck," a familiar voice said, and I turned and saw Sara, who looked ready to pop at any second. Extremely pregnant women make me nervous; it's like hanging around a ticking time bomb. "I'm sure you'll be fine. Where's the baby?"

I started to answer, when Michael said, "What baby?"

Seriously? He'd forgotten about BabyJon *again*? Okay, that was enough. Once this Council thing was taken care of, I was getting to the bottom of this. It was just too effing weird.

"Never mind," I said hurriedly before Sinclair, who looked decidedly bemused, could answer. "Can we just get going with this, please?"

"Of course." Michael gestured to two chairs, then turned on his heel and headed toward the front of the room. Derik materialized out of the crowd, said nothing to either of us, then grabbed Sara's hand and away they went.

I felt bad for him, to tell the truth. Grief was completely fucking him up—he was nothing like the easygoing blond fellow I had met earlier.

Worse, I knew that kind of grief was at least half guilt. He'd never forgive himself for not being there to save her. For not making her feel wanted *here*, so she wouldn't have moved away.

"All right, everyone. Attention, please." Michael didn't need a microphone; his voice carried perfectly, and the murmuring died down at once. "We're assembled here this evening to discuss the death of

Antonia Wolfton, who left our territory on a quest to the Midwest and never returned."

Well, hell. Anything sounded bad when you put it that way.

"Giving testimony tonight are Eric Sinclair and Elizabeth Taylor." I mentally groaned when he said my full name, and tried to ignore the snickers from the crowd. I cursed my mother under my breath for the zillionth time.

"They govern the vampire nation," Michael continued, "and have agreed to appear before the Council."

One by one, Michael introduced the Council members to us. I was a little surprised that they were all women—except for Michael. Maybe werewolves had a more, what d'you call it—matriarchal society?

Anyway, they ranged from middle-aged to elderly, all shapes and sizes. They took their seats at the big table up front, and the Q&A began.

Chapter 35

Dude, dude, dude.

I've been all over the mansion. Every room, every closet, every inch of the basement and the attic. The garage. The grounds.

I can't find Tina anywhere.

I don't know what to do.

I can't call the cops, for any number of obvious reasons. "Well, Officer, the devil's daughter has lost her mind, and is killing people who are already dead. She's doing it to keep her sister, the queen of the vampires, safe. Oh, her sister isn't here, she's on Cape Cod explaining to a bunch of werewolves why one of their own was shot to death in this very house. Sorry, we never got around to filing a police report. So could you get right on this, please?"

I can't call Betsy or Sinclair or Jess . . . no cell service.

Worse, I snuck out to buy one of those disposable phone cards, only to be intercepted by three—three—devil worshippers, who escorted me politely but firmly back to the mansion.

I hadn't realized she was spying on me. And dude, let me tell you—she's got people everywhere. She's even got one at Verizon—that's the one who was making sure our cells went down and stayed down.

Talking to Laura does no good at all. She just keeps giving me that big sweet smile and assuring me that everything she's doing is for Betsy's own good and really, maybe I should get more sleep because I seem awfully grumpy these days.

I can't call for help—Sinclair left the contact information with Tina.

And nobody's answering my e-mails.

Short of hopping on a plane bound for Logan, renting a car, driving to the Cape, and hoping I stumble across Betsy, Sinclair, and/or a werewolf, I'm out of ideas.

I even thought about nailing Laura with a trank,

except I'm pretty sure one or more of her Satan-worshipping followers would slaughter me like a goat.

As if things weren't bad enough, my admittedly bizarre home situation is starting to affect my work performance . . . I tried to admit a five-year-old to the geriatric ward last night. And don't even get me started on the poor woman who asked for the morning-after pill . . . I gave her a Tums.

I cannot believe things have gotten so bad, so quickly.

I'm out of ideas.

Chapter 36

ℓ was sitting at the front of the room, in what would be the witness chair if this was a courtroom. The Council was sitting to my left. Sinclair was right across from me, about ten feet away.

The room was jammed. Except for when Marc and I went to see Jim Gaffigan live, I'd never seen so many people in one place.

They were all perfectly silent. I could practically feel them all listening hard. It was like there were flies walking around in the back of my brain.

Through dumb luck I caught Sara's gaze and she smiled at me and nodded. If she'd been one of *them*, I might have taken some comfort from that. Well, at least there were two people in here who didn't want me to drop dead on the spot.

"And then what happened, Mrs. Sinclair?"

Oh, God, I'd almost forgotten the worst part. *They were calling me Mrs. Sink Lair!* Would the horror never end?

"Well," I said, ignoring my husband's grin, "we didn't know that the bad guy's son was behind everything. So we came back to the house and he was waiting for us. None of us saw him in time. He . . . uh . . ."

I stared down at my hands. "He was a cop. And he had a gun, of course. I think it was a .357."

"You're familiar with firearms, Mrs. Sinclair?"

"Yeah. My mom started taking me hunting with her when I was twelve."

"Very well. Please go on."

"Well. Like I said, nobody saw him in time. But then Antonia shoved me, really hard. I didn't—I didn't see her get shot. I just heard the shots. I think he emptied the gun into her. It was at least five shots for sure. And she—Antonia, I mean—she—uh—"

I clapped my hands over my eyes and told myself I wouldnotwouldnot*wouldnot* cry in front of these strangers, no chance, no way, ain't gonna happen.

So I burst into tears and said, "I didn't even know who was shot until I rolled her over. I thought—she was a werewolf and I thought you needed s-silver bullets or s-something like that, but she was just dead. There was blood and the stink of gunpowder, and we were all stuck in the hallway—there w-wasn't anywhere for us to g-go."

"That is *quite enough*." Sinclair was on his feet, his voice lashing through the ballroom like a whip. "My wife doesn't answer to the Council, or anyone here. Neither do I. We are here simply as a courtesy."

"It's fine, Sinclair," I said, which was just about the biggest lie ever. It was far from fine. But it was almost over. "There isn't much else."

"What happened to the man who shot at you?"

"He killed himself. Tucked the gun under his chin and pulled the trigger." I suddenly remembered a detail I'd managed to repress. "He used twenty-two longs."

The Council looked blank. I reminded myself that werewolves probably didn't have much to do with guns. "Those are special bullets that ricochet around inside a person for maximum damage, but they won't go through walls and kill an innocent bystander."

"Charming," one of the Council members muttered.

"And then what?" The head of the Council—the one who was asking most of the questions—seemed nice enough. Matronly, sort of. A headful of gray curly hair, big brown eyes. Laugh lines. And bifocals! I didn't know werewolves needed glasses.

"Then—then nothing. Antonia was dead. The bad guy was dead. So I called Michael and—and you know the rest."

"Why did you involve Antonia in vampire politics?"

"Involve her?" I asked blankly. "Involve her?" A shrill giggle burst out of me before I could squash it. "So, you never actually *met* Antonia, huh?"

There was an amused rustling from the assembled crowd, but I didn't score any points with the Council, who scowled at me as one.

"I only meant that Antonia did whatever the hell she liked. She wasn't afraid of anything, and she didn't take shit from anybody. Especially after she was able to change into a wolf during the—"

"*What?*" The Council spoke as one (creepy!) and there was an excited murmuring from the crowd.

The head cleared her throat, and the room hushed. "Mrs. Sinclair—"

"*Please* call me Betsy."

"Mrs. Sinclair, Antonia was a hybrid."

"Okay," I said.

"Meaning she couldn't change into a wolf. She had other gifts."

"Yeah, I know, she could tell the future. But see, she got kidnapped a while ago by a murderous librarian and when I rescued her and my husband—except he wasn't my husband then—I accidentally fixed it so she could change."

Dead silence.

"Uh . . . so can I go now?"

"You 'fixed it so she could change'?" the head of the Council asked, looking stunned. "What do you mean?"

"I—you know. I fixed it." How could I explain something I didn't understand myself? It seemed like I discovered a new weird power every other month.

I heard someone clear his throat, and then Michael was standing. "Mrs. Sinclair is quite correct. Antonia and I spoke frequently on the phone, and she explained to me that she was now able to change, thanks to the intervention of the vampire queen. In fact, Antonia was never happier in her life than she was in the final months with the Sinclairs."

My grip tightened on the arms of the chair as the room burst into noisy gabbling. Was this good for me or bad for me? I glanced at Sinclair, who simply raised his eyebrows at me. Fat lot of help he was.

"Michael, why didn't you bring this up while she was still alive?"

"Why?" I snapped. "So you could welcome her back now that she wasn't a freak in your eyes?"

"Mrs. Sinclair, no one is speaking to you right now."

"Too fucking bad. You guys aren't fooling *anybody*, you know. Pretty much everyone here made it clear they didn't want her around, so she left. Now she's dead, and you're trying to make it my fault, or my husband's . . . anybody's but the Pack's. Meanwhile you're playing the blame game while Antonia rots in her grave. And for what? So you don't feel bad? So you can make *me* feel bad? Trust me, nothing anyone says here today is going to hurt me more than I've hurt myself. You can't punish me more than I've punished myself."

Sinclair was nodding solemnly, as if listening to

something both wise and wonderful, but his hand was up, covering his mouth so no one could see him smile.

There was that feeling of flies in my brain again, and it took me a second to realize what was wrong. Before, the Pack had viewed me as an annoyance, a blundering idiot who'd gotten one of their family killed. Now they were seeing me as an active threat . . . who'd gotten one of their family killed.

Was this good for me, or bad for me?

The way my luck was going? Please. So, *so* bad for me.

Chapter 37

Betsy, you have to have to have to come home!
Laura has LHDM! Quit dicking around on
the Cape and CHRTM!

"You're right," Jessica said, squinting at the print-out of Marc's latest gabble. "It's pretty incomprehensible."

"I'm not answering him until he writes like a grown man instead of a thirteen-year-old girl. He knows how I feel about all the silly e-mail faux-netiquette garbage. And, hello? I've only got about fifty bigger problems to worry about."

"Yeah, I know. So finish already! You told the

Council that you gave Antonia more superpowers than she already had, and then what?"

"Then they decided to call it a night. I'm supposed to answer more questions later."

"Later, when? Tonight's the full moon."

"I know. I guess tomorrow night, maybe. Or—wait. Isn't the full moon usually for a couple of days?"

Jessica, who had been walking beside me down the beach, stopped and stared at me. I shifted BabyJon to my other arm and faced the dragon: "What? Something's on that so-called mind of yours. Spit it out."

"This is crap, Betsy," she said, kindly enough. "You've done everything they've asked. You did everything you could for poor Antonia, and then some. But because they found out you're a lot stronger than they ever imagined, they're assuming you can just hang out until they have everything settled their way? Bullshit."

"So, what? We leave before they're satisfied? How does that fix anything?"

"I don't know, but I sure don't like how you're letting them push you around."

"Well, they do sort of outnumber me seventy thousand to one."

"That's worldwide. There can't be more than three thousand on the Cape."

"Much better odds," I said glumly.

"Look, that's part of the reason I had to break up with Nick—"

I moaned and covered my eyes. "Something else to hate myself for."

"Oh, just stop it," she scolded. "I don't blame you—even if he does—and he made his choice."

"Yeah, but—don't you miss him?"

"Every day," she replied quietly. "But letting him stay in my life was going to cost too much. Even for me."

"I wish . . ." I trailed off. "I don't know. I wish for everything, I guess."

"You can't tell me Sinclair is fine with all of this."

"No, he's pissed. I mean, he got pissed during some of the questioning. Then he thought the rest of it was funny."

"Your husband is a whack job."

"Tell me. But that's not even my biggest problem right now."

"Split ends?" Jessica inquired.

"Shut your cake hole."

"Ah, cake. That reminds me, I missed lunch today."

"Can you stay focused, please?"

"Sorry, forgot—only for a minute—that everything's about you all the time."

"I've mentioned my deep hatred for you, right?"

"Twice today."

"What I'd like to know is what's the deal with my brother?" I patted BabyJon on his diapered rump. Sunset was about half an hour away. "Derik acts like BabyJon's head can spin all the way around, and Michael keeps forgetting I even brought a baby! Something is rotten in Hallmark."

"Denmark."

"Right."

"Don't take this the wrong way, Betsy, because I know you love him, but he *is* the spawn of the Ant and your dad. Who knows what twisted up his DNA?"

"That's fair enough," I admitted. We were slowly making our way from the beach to the mansion. "Especially when you consider the Ant's *other* kid."

"There's nothing wrong with Laura that getting laid wouldn't cure."

I started laughing so hard I nearly dropped the

baby. "That's quite enough about my siblings from you," I said, trying (and failing) to sound stern.

"Somebody's got to help you keep it real."

"Nobody's said 'keep it real' for about five years."

We walked through the front door and into the large receiving hall, and I still wasn't used to the immensity that was Wyndham Manor. It made our place in St. Paul look like an RV. I was about to comment on that to Jess when I noticed a bunch of people running toward us.

I instinctively clutched the baby—What now, for God's sake?—only to see them run straight past us.

"Betsy, oh my God! Look!"

I spun and looked. A kid—twelve? thirteen?—was falling, oh my God, he was actually *falling* from the third-level landing, headed straight for the marble floor. I thrust BabyJon at Jessica, but it was too late and the poor kid hit the floor with an awful, wet smack.

Chapter 38

Call an ambulance!" I screamed as a ring of adults surrounded the boy. "He's—what the *hell*?"

He was growling. At least three adults went reeling backward, and I saw a blurred face, lots of white teeth, a snarl of fur.

And the sounds, dear God, the *sounds*! It was the noise you'd hear coming from a slaughterhouse. Or if a cat was tossed into a pack of wild dogs. It was chilling; it was terrifying.

Suddenly Jeannie was there, hauling Jessica and me back by our elbows. "You need to go," she said firmly. "Now." She was practically carrying us; our heels were dragging across the floor. "Right now!"

"What—what's going on?" Jessica asked, trying to stare at the kid and extricate herself from Jeannie's grip while keeping her balance.

"He's only eleven. This is his first change. You need to leave right now. He won't be able to—"

More adults fell back. One of them spun right into Jessica, and she—oh my God, she—

She dropped my brother. Right in the path of a brand-new werewolf.

The crazed adolescent (was there any other kind?) charged at my brother and bit him. I screamed, high and shrill . . .

(Elizabeth? What's wrong?)

. . . and cried out for my brother, now surely dead at the hands of—

He was laughing.

BabyJon was laughing.

The new werewolf took off with his tail between his legs with at least three adults in pursuit, and suddenly the marble floor rushed up at me and hit me in the face.

Chapter 39

"... maybe she ..."

"... couldn't have ..."

"... her a minute ..."

"... just the shock ..."

I opened my eyes and saw Jeannie, Michael, Sinclair, and Jessica all peering down at me.

"Hey, there you are," Jess said. She was, thank God, holding BabyJon, who was wriggling and whining to come to me. "You fainted."

"I did not faint. Vampires don't faint."

"I know of at least one who does," Sinclair teased.

"What *happened*?" I asked, sitting up.

"We were hoping you could tell us," Michael said.

"Hey, one minute I'm minding my own business and the next some poor kid is falling to his death—except he didn't die—and then trying to eat my brother. Who appears to be not eaten."

In fact, BabyJon appeared to be fine. Which was impossible. I reached up and took him from Jess, inspected him, and found nothing except some saliva. No bite. No blood. Unbelievable.

"—don't normally go through their first change until thirteen or fourteen," Michael was saying. "Aaron's only eleven; nobody expected him to change during this phase."

"Is that why he did it while it was still daylight?" Jessica asked.

Nobody answered her, which was just rude. Super-Secret Werewolf Business, no doubt. And speaking of daylight, there wasn't much of it left. I imagine Michael was going to have to get furry pretty soon. Which meant—oh, shit.

"Sinclair!" I cried. "This castle is practically all windows, what the hell are you doing out of our room?"

He looked at me as if I'd suddenly grown another head. "You were screaming," he said simply. "In my head. I had to come."

"He jumped down from the third-floor landing," Jessica added. "I can't believe his femurs aren't in his lungs right now."

"Gross," was my only comment.

"I don't understand any of this," Michael said. "You said Aaron bit the baby? You must be mistaken; there isn't a scratch on him. And whose baby is that, anyway?"

Oh, for the love—

"Wait a second. Wait." Jessica frowned. She frowned harder. Her eyes went all narrow and squinty. Her lips twitched. Michael and Jeannie looked alarmed, but I knew that expression. It was her It's on the Tip of My Tongue look.

Then: "Bite him."

"What?"

"Bite the baby."

"Nobody's biting anybody's baby," I protested. "Least of all this one."

"I'll bite him," Jeannie offered.

Jessica shook her head. "It's got to be one of the vampires."

"Ah," Sinclair said. "I see what you're getting at."

"Swell," I grumped. "Somebody want to clue me in?"

"BabyJon may well be immune to dangers others would find crippling, even fatal."

"He's not immune to anything," I protested. "He's had colds. He's had shots at the pediatrician. He—don't do that!"

Sinclair, moving with the spooky speed that, even after all this time, startled the hell out of me, dipped his head and slashed at BabyJon with his jaws. He made a rattlesnake look slow.

I lashed out and punched him in the eye before I knew what I was doing. Then, when I did know what I was doing, I slapped at his shoulders. It probably looked to the others like he was on fire and I was trying to put him out. "What—do you think—you're doing?"

"Proving—ouch—Jessica's theory." He rubbed his eye. "Look."

"Look at *what*, you psychotic?"

"Look at the baby."

BabyJon yawned, unmoved by either a) the werewolf attack or b) the vampire bite.

"He doesn't have a mark on him!" Jeannie marveled. "That's the most amazing thing I've ever seen!"

"What, you're saying he's—what? Invulnerable?" I shook my head, feeling like I should be wearing a dunce cap. "But he's *not*. You guys know he's not. He's skinned his knee crawling, he's—"

"Invulnerable to paranormal harm," Sinclair said, and Jessica nodded.

"Wait a minute," Michael said. "That's *your* baby?"

"Well, look who just caught up. Seriously? You guys think that's what it is?"

"I saw Aaron try to bite him," Jeannie said quietly. "It would have killed a normal infant."

"When did you have a baby?" Michael asked, but I waved off his silly-ass questions.

"So that's why Derik kept freaking out around him. He knew something was different about Baby-Jon, but not what. And—Jeannie, how would a Pack leader deal with something he could never hurt?"

"Why . . . I suppose he would try to gain dominance of some sort," Jeannie replied slowly. "That's their nature. That's—"

"That's why Michael kept forgetting about BabyJon. He can't dominate someone if he doesn't remember him."

"How long has this baby been here?" Michael demanded, poor guy. He was sounding more and more bewildered . . . and the sun was dipping lower every second. Explanations would have to wait.

"We'll tell you all about it," Jeannie promised. "Later."

"When you aren't furry and drooly and such," I added.

"So a vampire can bite—and nothing will happen. A werewolf can chomp, a fairy can whack him with her wand—and nothing." Jessica paused, deep in thought. "Nothing at all. Wow."

"But why?" Jeannie asked. "Why would this baby be special?"

"It's a really long story," I said. "Which I'll probably never tell you."

Jeannie laughed. "That seems fair."

Chapter 40

Dude,

Not only is Tina gone, but her laptop is missing as well. I had hoped to use her e-mail address to get Betsy and Sinclair's attention, but a room-to-room search revealed nothing.

I was far too distracted at the hospital to do a reliable job, so I was taking unpaid sick time as I tried to figure out what the hell to do.

I managed to keep it casual as I asked Laura what she'd done with Tina's stuff, but just got another one of her insipid smiles and assurances that I didn't need to worry about a thing.

Ha. Worrying was more or less all I was doing.

And each time Laura tried to assure me she hadn't lost her mind, she sounded a little less sane.

"Marc, vampires are—with the possible exception of my sister—evil by nature. Betsy's life would be so much simpler if she didn't have to spend so much time policing monsters. And," she went on with the fervor of an evangelist, "not only am I helping Betsy, I'm keeping the peace in the Twin Cities, keeping the devil worshippers busy doing God's work—it's all good."

"Having me followed every minute of the day or night is God's work?"

She had the grace to flush a little at that. Maybe she wasn't entirely gone. "Marc, you don't know any better. You'll give Betsy all the wrong ideas. I want her to come home, too, but not until I've finished working on the surprise."

"The surprise? You mean there's more to come?" I tried not to sound as horrified as I felt.

"Sure! Lots more. You'll see, Marc. Besides, they're for your own protection. We can't have anything happen to you, now can we?"

"Will you at least consider the possibility that you've gone insane?" I asked, and got a soft laugh in response. She had thought I was kidding.

"You worry too much."

"What are you going to tell Betsy and Sinclair when they get back?"

"That I kept things safe for them," she replied promptly.

That you've gone looney tunes, I thought, but prudently kept that to myself.

I tried arguing with her for another ten minutes, and kept getting that sweet smile for a response. Dude, after a while I just wanted to whack that smirk off her face.

At least we still had an Internet connection, though what I knew about such things could be carried in an emesis basin. E-mails were about all I knew. Sure, I could have gone to an expert, a real techno geek . . . except I had Satan's Minions constantly on my heels.

In desperation I waited until she and the devil worshippers had left on another kill-all-vamps mission, then typed out a quick e-mail to Betsy. And sent it. And sent it. And sent it. And sent it.

Chapter 41

"Oh, there's my boy."

Jessica and I stared at each other, then Sinclair. It was almost two o'clock in the morning; the place was crawling with werewolves. I was a little curious and was interested in going outside, but Jessica was understandably nervous and had practically barricaded herself in the downstairs library.

And what a library! I swear, it was at least half the size of the New York City Public Library. Towering bookshelves, mahogany furniture, a row of computers . . . the only thing it was missing was a pair of stone lions.

Maybe it seemed larger because it had been empty

except for Jessica, me, and the baby. In fact, the mansion was practically deserted. But occasionally we could hear faint wolf howls from outside.

And now here was Sinclair bustling in and actually holding his arms out for BabyJon, formerly his number one rival for my affection.

"Your boy?" I asked, and Jessica raised her eyebrows.

"You know," Sinclair said, hovering over the baby and me, "it's not too soon to start planning his education."

"He can't even walk yet," Jessica pointed out.

"Oh, *I* get it. BabyJon is invulnerable to paranormal harm, so suddenly you're taking interest in his well-being."

"Elizabeth, you've got me all wrong." Sinclair had the nerve to look and sound wounded. "As your husband, and his coguardian, it's my responsibility to do right by this boy."

"Sure it is." I handed BabyJon over and Sinclair was so startled he juggled the baby for a few seconds before holding him at arm's length. "Okay, coguardian. He needs changing."

"Ah . . ."

"Don't even try to wiggle out of it," I warned.

"I've been dying to get out of here and walk around. Think you two can handle the kid for half an hour?"

"One of us can," Jessica said with a sly wink.

"Something smells awful," Sinclair moaned, and I practically sprinted out of the library before he could hear me laughing.

Chapter 42

It was a beautiful night—cool, with clear skies. The moon seemed to almost hang over Wyndham Manor, huge and white. There wasn't a cloud anywhere, and the stars seemed brighter and closer than they ever had been.

I started walking on the same path Lara and I had taken to the playground . . . Thanks to my vampire senses I could hear wolves running and walking and fucking all over the place. Two of them crossed my path, clearly playing Chase Me, but they moved so quickly I only got a blurred glimpse of tan fur and lots of teeth.

I must be out of my mind.

Well, that was always a possibility. But for once I wanted to take advantage of the fact that I, too, was fast and strong. I suppose if a few hundred of them ganged up on me I could be in serious trouble, but Jeannie had told me that werewolves didn't go feral during the full moon. They retained their human personalities, they just felt things more keenly. Sadness became depression; anger became fury; happiness became ecstasy. But no matter how deeply they felt something, innocent bystanders didn't get eaten.

Not that I was exactly innocent, but I think you know what I'm getting at. And it made sense—they had been coexisting with humans for millennia. People were bound to notice if gobs of mutilated corpses were found after each full moon.

I rounded the curve just in time to see the largest wolf I'd ever seen step out of the woods and block my path. Huge, with extremely light fur—almost white—and the biggest green eyes I'd ever seen. It was powerfully muscled and sat in the middle of the road, staring at me like a living statue.

"Uh, hello."

Nothing. Of course—what had I expected?

"I, uh, come in peace."

Then I realized where I'd seen those eyes before—
Derik.

Great. A werewolf who was pissed at me for getting his friend killed was now blocking my path. Ah, what a week!

I was suddenly so thirsty I could hardly stand it, but realized that was the vampire equivalent of adrenaline. The fight or flight reflex. The *last* thing I planned to do was bite him. It would be a novel way to be disemboweled.

"Good dog," I said, wishing I had a Milk-Bone. Or a case of them. "Uh—I wish Antonia was here with you right now. She was really happy when she was finally able to change."

Derik cocked his head, never blinking, and then—*ulp*—started walking toward me. Good-bye, cruel world.

He stopped at my feet and looked straight up at me. His head was bigger than a bowling ball. His paws were larger than my hand, even with all my fingers spread wide.

Is he gonna kill me?

Yup. He probably is.

Except he wasn't. He was just sitting there, staring up at me.

And all at once I stopped being nervous for myself and put myself in his shoes. Paws. His friend had died half a continent away, and he couldn't save her. Any more than I had been able to save her.

I knelt on the path. We were so close, our eyes were no more than eight inches apart.

"I am so sorry about Antonia," I said. "I'm sorry I couldn't save her. But you go on and stay mad at me, Derik. It's my fault she's dead. If I had it to do over, I'd have taken the bullets myself."

Derik threw back his head and howled—*shrieked*—at the moon. I thought my head was going to split. I thought my heart was going to split.

When I couldn't stand it another second, I flung my arms around his thick, furry neck. And did the thing I swore I wouldn't do again this week.

I cried and cried.

More wolves were padding out of the trees on either side of the road, one with Michael's black fur and distinctive golden eyes. They formed a ring around us, and the air was split again and again by the silvery, haunting howls.

Chapter 43

ℓ got back to our suite just before dawn. As I passed through the rooms, I checked on BabyJon—sound asleep. Thank God he hadn't been hurt—could never be hurt, at least by werewolves and vampires. He was *mine*. I wanted him to live forever.

Sinclair, with his usual brand of magic—or perhaps because he knew me so well—was waiting for me. I went to him without a word and hid my face against his shirt.

"Elizabeth, my own, my dear, shhhhh."

"It's all going wrong," I cried, "and I don't know how to fix it."

"This is very unbecoming to the ball-busting

queen I married," he said, trying to tease me into a smile.

"But I want to fix it!"

"You are young, my own."

I sniffled and looked up into his black eyes. "So?"

"So some things—many things—cannot be fixed. These people will have to be satisfied with your sorrow. You cannot give them any more of yourself."

"No, but I can give you more of myself."

I went up on tiptoe to kiss him and his mouth pressed over mine, his tongue darting and stroking. I slipped his suit jacket off his shoulders as his fingers were busy with my blouse buttons.

In another few moments we were naked and falling on the bed together. I was clutching at him, kissing him wildly, biting him, drawing blood even as he was drawing mine.

His teeth slid into my jugular just as that other part of him slid between my legs. I crossed my ankles behind his back and returned every thrust, every nip, every kiss.

I took everything. And gave back what I could.

Sometimes, I figured, that's all anyone can do, even if they *are* the queen of the vampires.

He held me for a long time, after.

Chapter 44

It was the next afternoon, late—close to five o'clock. Sinclair was up and working on the laptop (all the shades were drawn, natch). I was moping around, wondering what more the werewolves wanted, wondering how much longer I'd have to stay on the Cape to prevent a paranormal war.

"That's odd," Sinclair said.

"What now?"

"You've got several e-mails from Marc. Ah . . . thirty at least. And my damn cell phone still isn't working," he added in a mutter.

"Torturing me with more bad grammar and acronyms," I muttered. I was so not in the mood.

There was a polite rap at the door, and when I opened it, Derik and Michael were there.

"Okay to come in?" Derik asked, looking a little more like his old self.

"Ask him," I said nodding at Michael. "It's his house."

"Yes." Michael smiled at me. "We can come in."

Sinclair came into the sitting room, nodded politely and, seeming to know what was up, excused himself to give us a false sense of privacy (with his hearing, there *was* no privacy . . . not when we were only twenty feet away).

"I, uh, wanted to apologize," Derik said stiffly. "About before."

"You don't have to."

"I do have to, not least because if I don't, it'll get me in trouble with my wife."

I laughed. "When is she due?"

"Any second."

"Yeesh." I've mentioned hugely pregnant women make me nervous, right? "Well, good luck with all of that."

"I wanted to tell you that the Council is satisfied with your testimony and thanks you for your cooperation."

I was silent. I wasn't the smartest woman in the world, but even I could smell Derik all over that one. Sometime today, when he woke up with two legs instead of four, he had fixed things with the Council.

"Thanks," I said. "I'm glad you—I'm glad the Council is satisfied."

"On a more personal note," Michael said, giving me the friendliest smile I'd ever seen, "my home and my lands are open to you and your husband anytime. I hope you'll come to see us again soon."

"Oh. Well, thanks." "Thanks" seemed big-time inadequate, but it was all I could come up with.

Poof! Just like that, our troubles were over. It was hard to believe that we could just pick up and leave without werewolf repercussions.

Sinclair rapped politely, then came into the room and handed me a hard copy of one of Marc's e-mails. It was such a disaster it actually hurt my brain to look at it.

Betsy!
  CBN grrrl Laura's LHM and IDKWTD!!!!!
Please you have to GYBBH ASAP! I am so not
LOLing right now please please come!

"It's the same message over and over."

I rolled my eyes. "Who can make heads or tails of this? Maybe we should call him."

"I have been. Nobody answers . . . and I can't reach Tina."

Huh. That was odd. Tina was available to Sinclair at all times.

Derik peeked over my shoulder. "Holy crap. You'd better get going."

"What?" I looked at the gibberish. "You mean you actually understand this mess?"

"You mean you don't? 'Come back now, girl. Laura's lost her mind and I don't know what to do. Please, you have to get your butt back home as soon as possible! I am so not laughing out loud right now. Please, please come!' "

There was a short silence as Sinclair and I locked gazes. He looked as horrified as I felt.

"Oh my God. Oh my—get Jessica. Get the baby. We have to go right now—oh my God, what's she done? Did she lose it and kill Tina?"

"You've got trouble at home," Michael said, not wasting our time with silly questions. "Is there anything we can do to help?"

"I'll come with you, if you want," Derik offered.

"*No*, that's—that's okay. I mean, thanks and everything, but you stay here with your wife. Sinclair, Jessica's got to call Cooper and get the plane ready." I was dashing around the room, scooping up clothes and flinging them in the general direction of one of the suitcases.

"I've got some people at the airport," Michael said. "I'll call ahead and make sure you're not unnecessarily delayed."

"Great. That's great. Okay, let's—damn! I almost forgot."

"Forgot what?"

"Your mom says not to name your daughter after her."

"My—*what*?"

"Your mom."

"My mom's been dead for twenty—"

"I know. But that doesn't change the fact that she doesn't want another Theodocia running around in the world."

That was how we left Antonia's best friend and the Pack leader: amazed and staring after us.

Chapter 45

I wasn't sure how Cooper had managed to shave thirty-five minutes off our flight time, and I didn't want to know. Sinclair's car was waiting on the tarmac for us when we landed, and the four of us piled in and took off.

Sinclair made that car *move*, getting us to the mansion in record time. Before we could even get to the front door, it was yanked open and Marc was framed in the doorway.

"It's about damned time!"

"If you wrote your emergency messages in English, we would have been back three days ago. Where's Laura? Where's Tina? What's going on?"

"I haven't seen Tina in days. I think Laura might have done something."

We followed him through the house. "What's she been doing?"

"You might as well see for yourself. Because even I don't believe it, and I've *seen* it."

He stiff-armed the door to the parlor, which swung open.

Sinclair, Jessica, and I stared at the goings-on.

He was right. I didn't believe it.

Chapter 46

The parlor was packed with people in dark hooded robes. Laura was standing at the front of the room, holding a clipboard.

"Okay, then after you take care of the two vampires who got away last night, I need some of you back here. I was able to intercept a call to the house—I guess some vampires from Maine are on their way to pay tribute." Laura shook her head. "Blasphemy. Then we'll—"

"What the *fuck* are you doing?"

Laura glanced up, startled, and instead of looking ashamed or scared or sad, she looked delighted.

"Betsy! Thank goodness you're back. I've got so much to tell you."

"Why," I demanded, "are you meeting with monks in our house in the middle of the night?"

"Those aren't monks," Marc sighed. "They're devil worshippers."

"Devil—" I suddenly realized what was going on. They were confusing Laura with her mother. But why would Laura have anything to do with—

"Laura," Sinclair said in a calm tone that didn't fool me at all, "where is Tina?"

"Oh, I had to get her out of the way," Laura said with Bambi-like sincerity. "She would have tried to stop me. But I'm being rude. Everybody, this is my sister, Betsy, and her husband, Sin—"

"We don't need intros!" I snapped. "We need to find out where Tina is." *Not to mention when you lost your mind.*

"I'm in a meeting right now," she said in a scolding mommy voice. "I don't—"

I hauled one of the robed morons to his—his? yep, it was a guy—feet and tossed him away. He bounced off the wall like he was a SuperBall, hands clapped to his face as his nose gushed blood.

"I want you athholth out of my houth!"

"Protect the Beloved of the Morningstar!" some other hooded freak yelled, and just like that, I had my hands full.

Chapter 47

Dude,

Thank God, thank God, thank God, Betsy finally came home and she brought the cavalry. I was torn between the urge to strangle her because she took so long, and hugging her because I was so relieved.

They caught Laura practically red-handed, which was even better, because it saved a lot of time.

Unfortunately, Laura not only wasn't sorry, she wasn't even defensive. She seemed proud and happy that she had found a way to "help" Betsy, and the more she talked about the vampires she and her minions had killed, the more pissed Betsy and Sinclair got.

I've never been particularly scared of Betsy, but Sinclair was a whole different story. Even when he was pleasant, he could be sort of terrifying. And he wasn't being pleasant now.

I managed to haul Jessica aside and told her to get her ass out of here and take the baby with her—something fairly awful was about to happen, and I didn't want either of them to get hurt.

Jessica must have believed me, because she didn't make so much as a token protest. Just picked up the diaper bag, the baby in the car seat, and left.

Which left Laura, the devil worshippers, me, Betsy, and Sinclair. That's when things started to get a little on the violent side.

When Betsy shoved one of the devil worshippers she gave him a bloody nose, so her fangs popped (you can always tell—she lisps, which is hilarious under most circumstances). And of course Laura felt obliged to protect her minion. Which is when the rest of them jumped us.

I still couldn't believe how quickly things had gone to shit. I should never have suggested to Laura that she find ways to work with the misguided morons who kept showing up.

Everything was my fault.

Chapter 48

I had just enough time to grab Marc by the collar, ignore his surprised squawk, and bundle him into the closest closet. The poor guy looked ghastly—pale, with dark circles under his eyes and at least three days of stubble. Clearly he'd been under stress during our little sojourn to the Cape. And no wonder, with the devil's daughter cracking up right under his nose.

As usual, things were happening so quickly I was having trouble keeping up. Even as a bunch of jerks in hoods rushed me, Sinclair was there, knocking and shoving and punching them out of the way.

Which left me free to—

"Laura!"

Her big blue eyes, wide, got even wider as I hit her around the thighs in a low tackle. I knocked her backward a good four feet, and she slammed, back first, into the far wall of the parlor.

"Betsy, have you lost your mind?" Crazy Lady had the nerve to ask. "Get off!"

"What'd you do with Tina, nut job?"

"Oh, I like that! After everything I've done for you, you can't even show me simple gratitude."

"Gratitude?" I almost gagged on the word. "Thank you for going crazy? For killing our subjects and maybe even our friend? I'd like to put your fucking head through a wall."

"Like this?" she asked brightly and, cat-quick, she wriggled free of me, seized a yank of my hair, and drove me face-first into the wall.

My face blew up. Or at least, that's what it felt like. My nose was already dripping, and I was pretty sure there was a piece of wallpaper in one of my eyes.

Will you get it together? You're undead; she's not. You're stronger and faster; she's not.

As I reminded myself of essential facts of nature, Laura picked me up like a wolf with a cub and heaved me so hard I crashed through the wall and spilled into the next room.

I shook splinters out of my hair, wiped the blood from my face, and reassessed the situation. Clearly, Laura had been keeping secrets. Or had never come up with a tactful way to explain she had superhuman strength.

Which was my own fucking fault. She *was* the Antichrist, after all.

I'd even seen the breakdown coming. I'd just kept conveniently shoving it out of my mind. It seemed like there was always something more important claiming my attention: killing the old vampire king, my wedding, catching serial killers, my wedding, catching a crooked cop, my wedding . . . and now I was paying the price.

Worse, I wasn't paying it alone.

"After everything I've done for you," Laura said reproachfully, standing and brushing bits of wall off her sweater. "Clearly the undead have been a terrible influence on you."

"And clearly your mother's been one on you."

As soon as it was out, I wished I could take it back. Because right in front of my eyes, Laura's mouth went thin and hard, and her hair turned red.

Never a good sign.

Chapter 49

Dude,

Betsy bundled me so efficiently and so quickly into the closet, I hardly had time to protest. And believe me, dude, the irony of me being *back in the* closet was not lost on me.

I hammered on the door, wanting to help them any way I could, but she must have jammed the knob with a chair or something.

Great. My friends were going to live or die ten feet from me, and I was helpless. I'd been *helpless this entire week. No matter what I did, or tried, things just kept getting worse.*

I'd been so happy to see Betsy and Sinclair. Now I wished I'd kept my mouth shut and kept them far, far away.

Chapter 50

"Think about what you're doing, Laura."

"I told you never to speak of her around me." She was striding forward and I was backing up—while trying to tell myself I wasn't backing up. Laura's hair went red when she was indulging a homicidal rage. My little sis definitely had a dark side.

"Can't we talk this through—oooooh!"

This time I crashed, back first, into the fireplace. Luckily it was a mansion-sized fireplace, not the little ones you usually see in houses these days. The thing was big enough to roast a sheep in. Or a vampire.

"All right, enough is fucking enough." I crawled,

coughing soot, out of the fireplace. "No more Mrs. Nice Guy. I'm not pulling any more—" That was as far as I got before I had to duck. Laura's clenched fist whistled over my head and went right into the wall.

She hissed in pain, yanked her hand free, and whipped around so fast she'd given me an eye-watering slap before I knew what was happening.

"This isn't striking you as just a little bit psychotic?" I asked. Too bad Laura wasn't bleeding; I could really have used my fangs about now.

"*You're* the psychotic. Running around saving vampires instead of killing them, it's nonsense."

"I've killed some vampires," I whined.

"*I* have been trying to save your soul."

We were stalking each other, circling warily. "My soul's fine. But *you* need to be on medication."

I could hear tons of racket from the other room— Sinclair, taking on the thirty or so devil worshippers by himself. I couldn't help him; I could only pray he wouldn't get badly hurt.

"I destroy evil, so I should be medicated?"

"You've appointed yourself judge, jury, and executioner."

"They're vampires!"

"So am I. Are you going to kill me, too?"

"No," she said sulkily. "At least, I don't think so."

"Laura, what's *wrong* with you? What happened while we were gone?"

"Marc gave me an epiphany."

"What is that, an STD?"

She rolled her eyes. "He solved a big problem for me. He showed me the light."

"I'll show you a light." I seized her by the hair (cat fight!), yanked her down sharply, and brought my knee up into her nose, which broke with a soft crunch.

Laura screamed. My sister was screaming. And bleeding. Here came my fangs—at the worst possible time. Just what Laura needed to see—a physical reminder that I was one of the evil beings she was trying to wipe off the planet.

I brought my hand up to hide my lips. "Laura, I think if we dithcuth thith, we can—"

Something bright swung toward me, something that shone like a small sun, something that hurt to look at. I ducked . . . and Laura's Hellfire sword whistled over my head.

Oh, this was getting better and better. First, the psychotic break. Then the red hair. Now her weapons. Laura could pull a sword, a crossbow, whatever, out of thin air and no matter what shape the weapon took, it was fatal to vampires.

And their queen.

Chapter 51

Dude,

The door actually split down the middle and, with judicious shoving, I freed myself . . . and promptly tripped over two unconscious devil worshippers.

Sinclair was a whirl of activity; I could only get the occasional glimpse of him when he managed to knock a bad guy away from him. And I realized why the door had been broken—he'd thrown someone into it so hard, the flimsy closet door had cracked.

I tried to figure out who to help. Calling the cops was out, for obvious reasons. Getting between Betsy and Laura would be a quick and painful way to commit suicide.

So when a hooded jerk ran past me I caught him by the back of his robe, yanked him back, and smashed my elbow into the hinge of his jaw.

"That'll teach you to mess with a licensed physician," I told the unconscious Satanist.

Then I ran to see if I could give Sinclair a hand.

Chapter 52

I ducked again as her Hellfire sword whistled over my head, and sidestepped so quickly I tripped over a chair. I was in such a hurry to scramble to my feet that for a few seconds I ran in place, like the Road Runner.

Then I was up and backing away again.

"You came back too soon," Laura said, circling me. Her knuckles were white on the sword hilt. If my eyes could water, they would have. It was like she was holding the sun.

"Tell me about it," I retorted. And I thought I had problems on the *Cape*? Good God, I didn't know what problems *were*. "I should have left BabyJon in charge."

"You never mind about him."

"Your mother infected him, too," I said brightly as a wonderful idea came to me.

"You shut up."

"Yep. He's got demonic unholy powers—just like you!"

"I said. *Shut. Up.*"

"You know what they say . . . like mother, like dau—"

She forgot about the sword and, the minute she wasn't concentrating on it, it disappeared . . . back to hell, or whatever unholy armory her weapons came from.

She hooked her long, slender fingers into claws and ran straight at me. They looked very long and very sharp. And pink! Blech.

I managed to grab her by the wrists and keep her hands away from my face. Sure, it was a cliché, but she really was trying to dig her fingers into my eye sockets.

We danced around in a tight, difficult circle, me holding on to her wrists for dear life—getting killed was one thing, but having my eyeballs clawed out was something else again—and her straining to mess up my pretty face in all sorts of nasty ways.

"Can't—we—just—get—along?" I managed.

"You go to hell," she snapped.

"But I don't want to see your mom anytime soon."

"Stop calling her that!"

"Fine. I don't want to see the fallen angel who gave you life. See? I didn't use the *M* word."

She yanked me forward, which I wasn't expecting, and gave me a savage head butt. Stars actually exploded behind my eyes and I sagged in her grip.

Which is when she picked me up and threw me out the window.

I heard the glass shatter but, fortunately, didn't feel it. Mostly because my entire face had gone numb. When the *hell* had Laura learned to fight dirty?

I'd actually thought I could take her, reasoning that I'd been in more fights than she had. It was only about the tenth time I'd underestimated the Big Bad.

I hit the lawn with a teeth-rattling thud, thought about passing out for a few seconds, then painfully climbed to my knees.

Where I spotted the feet.

Clad in Vera Wang strappy gold sandals in mint condition.

Only one creature in the galaxy has such great shoes.

I flopped over on my back and stared up into the devil's smiling face.

Chapter 53

"Hello, Betsy," Satan said cheerfully. "Having a bad week?"

"You," I groaned.

"Yes, me. That's it? That's the best you can do? You were never the sharpest knife in the drawer, Betsy, when it came to rejoinders."

"Fuck rejoinders. This is your fault. You drove Laura crazy."

"I certainly did not." The devil had the nerve to look offended. She was a petite woman with gray-streaked hair pulled back in a bun. Her navy blue suit ruffled, showing her indignation.

"Did, too."

"No, I stayed well away from Laura." The devil smiled, revealing dimples. "I might have, however, said a word or two in Dr. Marc Spangler's ear."

"Oh, man," I said. It occurred to me I was still lying on the lawn, broken glass everywhere, bleeding, and Satan was standing over me.

Yep. Things could not get any worse.

That's when Marc came sailing out the same window and landed right on top of me.

Chapter 54

Marc squashed me so thoroughly it was a damned good thing I didn't need to breathe much. I lay on the grass like a landed trout, my mouth opening and closing, shoving and pushing at his carcass.

"Betsy," Marc said, remarkably unharmed. Of course, I'd broken his fall. Stretch some rubber over me and call me a trampoline. "This is all my fault."

"It's not," I wheezed.

"No, really, it is. I—"

"Marc, do you think you could get the hell off me sometime today?"

He leaned back, squashing just one lung now. "I'm the one who—"

"It's not your fault. Marc, this is Satan. Satan, this is—"

"I know Dr. Spangler, thank you."

Marc was gaping up at the devil. "Satan? Laura's mother, Satan? *That* Satan?"

"How many do you know?" I pushed him the rest of the way off me and climbed slowly to my feet. "We're the flies in her web, as usual."

The devil shook her head. "I never interfere with free will."

"No, but you're sure good at inspiring it. I've got to get back in there."

"But we were having such a nice talk. Where are you going?"

"I'm gonna go tell Laura what you did."

The devil raised a dark eyebrow. "You're going to tattle on the devil?"

"Damn right!"

I began the painful climb back up through the window, pausing just long enough to tell Marc, "Will you for God's sake get the hell out of here? Somebody's likely to get killed and I'd rather it wasn't you."

I'd rather it wasn't me, either, but I wasn't placing any bets on that one.

Chapter 55

Dude,

You are not even going to believe what happened next. I was there, and I hardly believe it myself.

I pulled another one of the hooded jerks off Sinclair—there appeared to be an unending supply—but one of them fell back so fast he knocked me through a window. It was a little like being in a Western. The window, luckily, had already been broken.

By Betsy, whom I landed on. It was the closest thing to straight sex I'd experienced in years. Although I have to say, she was more bony than lush. It was those long femurs of hers.

Betsy, clearly squashed, managed a weak groan.

I tried to explain what had happened, which is when she introduced me to the devil. The *devil*. Then she (Betsy) scrambled back through the window.

I decided there was a strong possibility that I was concussed, and reminded myself to watch for symptoms. Surely this was the result of a mind weakened by blunt-force trauma.

"So, Marc. Let's talk. How have you been?"

I gaped at her. This was Lucifer? The Fallen One? Samael? The Morningstar? She looked like a beautiful middle-aged, gray-streaked brunette with pretty shoes. And those ankles! I was getting straighter and straighter by the moment.

"What do you want with us?"

"Nothing at all." The devil gazed thoughtfully at the broken window. "Laura's my primary interest. The rest of you—you're just wrenches in the toolbox of life. Things to use. Tools."

"That was a terrible analogy."

The devil gave me a decidedly unfriendly look.

"Why don't you just leave Laura alone, to live her own life?"

"Dear boy. Even mothers who aren't *me* can't do that for their children."

250

"She could have a happy life if you'd just leave her alone."

Satan snorted through her nose. "Leave her alone? Never! She's been poisoned by humanity. She actually thinks what happens to other people matters. I have the cure for that diseased worldview."

I stood, brushing grass off my knees. "I don't like you one bit."

"Ooooh." The devil smirked. "That one hurt. By the way, Marc, he knows."

"What?"

"Your father. He knows all about you." She leaned forward and whispered in my ear, "He has always known. Oh, Marc. How you've disappointed him. You should see him cry when he's alone and thinks no one's watching. Like you do, sometimes."

A sliver of ice pushed its way into my gut, but before I could think of a retort, or run away, the devil was gone.

Leaving the rest of us, of course, to clean up the mess she had instigated.

Chapter 56

Laura looked delighted to see me crawl back into the room. "Good. I was hoping to beat the sin right out of your silly vain carcass, and I wasn't sure I had finished the job."

"Your mother's in the yard."

Laura, already reaching for my throat, hesitated. "Don't lie, Betsy. You've tried everything but that."

"But she is. I just talked to her. She said she gave Marc the idea about how you could use your followers to kill vampires."

"That isn't true." But she didn't look at all sure of herself. "Marc would never hurt me."

She reached for me again and I batted her hand

away. "He's not the one out to push your buttons, dumbass! *She* is. This is, like, phase five of her plan to have you take over hell when she retires."

My ears rang and I realized she'd slapped me so hard and fast that I'd barely seen her hand move. "Stop talking about her!"

"Laura, she *wants* you to do everything you're doing."

"That's not true! I've been doing good! We've been killing demons!"

"No, you've been suckered. If you won't stop for my sake, or your own, then stop for no other reason than because it will completely foil your mother's wicked-ass plans for you."

Here came the bright light. Here came the sword, straight for my heart. Here came the killing blow, and thank goodness, because one way or the other, it meant the fight was almost over.

I sidestepped and punched Laura in the eye. She went down without a sound.

I didn't realize until it was too late that she'd swung wide on purpose.

Chapter 57

Sinclair staggered through the doorway, looking like he'd been through a hurricane. Or through a whole shitload of devil worshippers. Having vampire strength and reflexes was all fine and good, but it didn't mean that enough bad guys couldn't take a piece or two out of you.

His suit was in tatters; his face was streaked with blood. I imagine I didn't look much better. At least we were both standing. Well, leaning.

"Some of them are dead," he informed me. "Some of them ran off."

Marc called from the other room, "And some

of them are going to need medical attention! I'll do what I can."

Sinclair took in the ruined room, the holes in the walls, the broken windows, Laura, unconscious on the floor.

"Are you all right?"

"Shit, no. But I'll live. How about you? You look like somebody dropped you into a blender and pressed *puree*."

"What a coincidence. That is precisely how I feel."

I went to him and hugged him, closing my eyes as he stroked my back. "Laura's mom was here."

"That explains much."

"It explains mucher than you know."

"At least you won the fight."

I looked up at him. "She could have killed me at any time. She threw the fight when she realized her mother had been pulling her strings all this time."

"Ah."

"Yeah."

I imagined Sinclair didn't need me to spell out the ramifications for him. Given the way he was grinding his teeth, I knew he was equal parts pissed for me and frightened for me.

Because if Laura could kill me anytime—she'd hidden her strength and speed all this time, for one thing—who was really in charge around here? A mere vampire?

Or the devil's daughter?

And what about the next time Laura and I butted heads? Much as I hated to admit it, there most likely *would* be a next time. I couldn't count on her to throw every fight. Frankly, I was pretty sure she'd only thrown this one because I'd shocked her with the bald truth. There were only so many times I could play the sister card.

And next time, she wouldn't be taken off guard.

Next time, she might kick my ass straight into hell, and then bye-bye for every vampire she could get her hands on.

And she could get her hands on a lot. Especially since she apparently had followers who would do whatever she asked. Legions of them.

It should have been over.

But it wasn't. We'd earned a temporary respite, that was all.

Chapter 58

$\mathcal{B}$etween Marc and Sinclair, they pulled enough strings to get the wounded to the hospital without us having to fill out reams of paperwork or answer unanswerable questions. Not for the first time I appreciated being married to a rich man who knew people . . . not to mention having Dr. Spangler as a roommate.

Sinclair carried Laura to the room she'd been staying in and laid her on the bed. She was going to have an unattractive shiner, but Marc checked her over and pronounced her merely unconscious.

We still had no idea where Tina was, so I stayed

in the room listening to Laura's soft breathing, waiting for her to wake up.

After about half an hour, her eyes opened and she stared at the ceiling, then at me.

"Welcome back."

"Is it true?" she asked hoarsely, and I realized with a stab of pity that she was afraid. "Did my mother have something to do with all this?"

"Yeah, Laura. It's true."

"I was so sure it was a good plan, the right plan. Instead of running from those—those people, I thought I was—oh, Betsy! How am I ever supposed to know what's my idea, and what's part of her plan for me?"

The time was past for comforting lies. "I don't know."

"I'd rather be dead than be her puppet."

"Can't we find a happy medium between those two?"

She suddenly seemed to notice my ruined suit, the blood, my mussed hair, the way I was covered with bits of soot, wallpaper, and plaster.

Her face crumpled and she clapped her hands over her eyes. I leaned forward, grasped her wrists, and gently pulled her hands away from her face.

"Come on, Laura. It's not fatal. This is why God

invented dry cleaners. Also, it's going to be really, really awkward between us for a while. It might even ruin Christmas."

My lame-ass joke fell flat—deservedly so—and Laura burst into tears. "I'm sorry," she managed, pulling free of my grip. "I'm just so, so sorry."

She rested her forehead on my shoulder and I stroked her (blond) hair while she sobbed all over my already filthy suit. "It's all right, Laura. We'll figure it out. Come on, enough with the waterworks."

"I could have killed you."

"But you didn't." You just killed a bunch of my people. But I'd have to address that later. I wasn't looking forward to it, that was for damned sure. "You let me hurt you—punch you out like we were brawlers in a Western—rather than killing me. You know what that makes you?"

"No."

"One of the good guys. Your white hat is in the mail."

"No, it's not," she said again, and wept harder.

Chapter 59

Traffic was light at this time of night, and Sinclair rode the gas pedal like he was in the race of his life. Which wasn't far off.

In next to no time (objectively, subjectively it seemed to take a week), we were at Laura's apartment in Dinkytown, opening the door to the spare bedroom.

Marc, Sinclair, and I all stared. Laura was studiously *not* staring.

Finally I said, "Devil worshippers brought a coffin up here and nobody noticed?"

Laura shrugged. I moved forward and stripped the crosses off the coffin, off the inside door handle, and the windows—no wonder Tina had disappeared from the picture so completely. The crosses were more effective than bear traps.

I popped the top off of the second coffin in the same week. "Hey, Tina? Rise and shine, it's time to—*gggkkk*!"

Tina's hands had shot up and out and she was briskly strangling me while I gurgled and grabbed her wrists. "Help me, you idiots," I choked, which seemed to break the spell . . . Marc and Sinclair both sprang forward to prevent Tina from snapping me in half.

The perfect end to a perfect week.

They pulled her off me and Sinclair helped her sit up. She was terribly wasted, terribly *old,* but I knew some blood would fix her right up. She kept beating her withered hands at Sinclair's shoulders and trying to speak.

"Be calm, Tina."

"Yeah, be calm already," I added. "We'll take care of you."

"Laura," she whispered, so faintly I had to strain to hear. "You have to watch out for Laura."

"They know," Laura said, staring at her shoes.

Then Sinclair *and* Marc *and* I had our hands full keeping Tina from ripping out my sister's throat and taking a shower in the blood.

Chapter 60

"Oh, come on, you guys." Everyone but Laura was in our kitchen . . . it was the next evening, and I didn't think Tina was going to *not* try to kill my sister anytime soon. And who could blame her? Laura had tricked her, trapped her, and starved her. Something other than a Hallmark card was definitely called for. "We won! The bad guys are vanquished. Why so glum?"

Sinclair was giving Marc his "you idiot" stare, but Marc was so happy we were all back home he was overlooking a few things.

Sure, we had friends among the werewolves now . . . including Michael and Jeannie, which was quite a coup. I could practically hear Sinclair trying to figure out how to turn their goodwill to our advantage.

And yes, we'd found out BabyJon was no ordinary baby—which was a great relief, given our dangerous lifestyles. If he was going to be raised by vampires, it was excellent that he couldn't be hurt by them.

The vampires Laura and her minions had killed were all pretty bad characters . . . Sinclair and Tina knew each and every name, and couldn't deny the planet was better off without those particular undead walking around.

However, the ends don't justify, et cetera.

Worse, I didn't think Laura had learned her lesson. She had never regretted killing the vamps, she only regretted hurting me. There was still work ahead.

The only thing worse?

She threw the fight. She let me win. *Let* me. Which meant she could probably kill me whenever she wanted. If the devil decided to whisper in the wrong ear again, I could be in very serious trouble.

But even if that never happened (ha!), I had discovered something new and awful about my sister.

Despite my earlier assurance, Laura wasn't necessarily a good guy. In fact, I was pretty sure she was the worst kind of bad guy. She was a bad guy who *thought* she was a good guy.

I was normally pretty sanguine about the future, but I wasn't going to be able to relax for a while.

I didn't think any of us were.

Chapter 61

Dude,

This will be my last entry for a while. I think part of the reason I wrote so much this week was because Sinclair and Betsy weren't here, and it helped fill my days.

They're back now, and things are sort of back to normal. Tina's still not speaking to Laura. Laura's avoiding all of us. BabyJon apparently has superpowers. And Betsy doesn't seem quite so bubble-headed.

Only Sinclair is the same: cool, calculating, untroubled. Thank God he loves Betsy—I'd hate to think what would happen to us if he didn't.

Meeting the devil—that was a new one for me, even for the funhouse we all live in.

I can't get what she said out of my head.

So I'm going to call my dad tonight. Maybe even go see him.

The devil might have told me he knew my secret to fuck me up, and that's fine—that's the devil's job.

I plan to use the information to make my life—and maybe my dad's—a little better.

That ought to fix that rotten bitch. And hey, Satan, since you're so busy watching me, let me be the first to say: not even those Vera Wangs can hide the fact that Lena's got better ankles than you.

Later, dude.

And now, a sneak preview of

Undead and Unfinished

the ninth installment of
the Betsy the Vampire Queen series
by MaryJanice Davidson.

𝓛 would never have gone to Hell in the first place if the Antichrist hadn't been fluent in Tagalog. Talk about your perfect storm of paranormal weirdness . . . and on Halloween, too.

Okay, so, I'll back up. This whole mess started simply enough (they always, always do): Bloomingdale's was having a shoe sale, and for once, the retail time warp worked in my favor.

Okay, I'll back up more. You know how stores are actually about four months ahead of the actual calendar? Like Halloween decorations on sale the day after Easter? (Pardon me while I embrace the horror.) Like that. So anyway, even though it was

Halloween, they were having their spring shoe sale (because when there's a foot of snow on the ground, everybody wants to buy sandals, right?). And the Antichrist asked if she could tag along, so I said okay.

I . . . said . . . okay! You'd think I hadn't been paying attention the last four years. How could I not see the coming disaster? It shouldn't have mattered that the Antichrist needed a new pair of loafers. I should have realized that an innocent quest for fine leather footwear would have ended up with me in Hell and the Antichrist freaking out. Again.

Right. The Antichrist. I should probably explain that, too. My half sister, Laura, was fathered by my, uh, father. Dear Old Dad was banging away at my stepmother, the wretch formerly known as Antonia and whom I had always called the Ant, and didn't notice she was possessed by Satan. I'm betting devil-possessed Ant isn't any worse than non-devil-possessed Ant, which is a sad commentary on my father's taste in second wives.

The thing is, Satan hated pregnancy, delivery, and breast-feeding. So she did the whole "baby on the doorstep" thing and beat feet back to Hell.

So my sister, who was raised by a minister, is not

only the Antichrist, it's been foretold she'll take over the world. Possibly between donating blood and teaching Sunday school.

But! I will be the first to admit, the Antichrist is *nice*. Works in homeless shelters, runs blood drives (kind of hilarious, given that her sister, namely *moi*, is a vampire), makes cupcakes for church bake sales. Chocolate ones. With real buttercream frosting. *Buttercream*, not the colored Crisco that grocery stores try to pass off as frosting. Mmm.

Of course, Laura's got a temper. Who doesn't? And occasionally she loses it and then slaughters anyone she can get her hands on. That gets awkward, kind of. And she's totally conflicted about the undead. Which is actually a pretty normal reaction to vampires.

Her temper and occasional forays into psychopathic rage were why we were meeting tonight at the Mall of America. Laura had sort of tried to kill me a couple of months ago, and still felt crummy about it. She detested conspicuous consumerism and also shopping, which is why her offer to go to my personal Graceland was an olive branch.

I had risen from my unholy grave (bed, actually, with navy blue flannel sheets from Target—it

271

was October), devoured an innocent for breakfast
(a tripleberry smoothie; a perk of being the Queen
of the Undead was that I didn't have to suck down
blood every day, though to be honest, I always
wanted to), then commandeered my sinister chariot
(Ford Hybrid Escape) and went mallward bound.

I parked in the East Parking Lot, second floor—
lots of my favorites were on that side, including
Williams-Sonoma and Coach—not that I'd ever
cough up four hundred bucks for a knapsack that
looked like it was designed by a bright second grader.
Also, Tiger Sushi was there, and Laura was seriously
addicted to their Tiger Balls.

Yeah, I can read you like a book, pal. Grow up.

So I forced a smile as I marched toward a restaurant that sold seaweed, rice, and raw fish for a profit
margin of several hundred percent. The sushi thing.
I didn't get it and I never would. I'd gone fishing too
much as a kid; I couldn't make myself eat bait, no
matter how fresh it was.

I spotted Laura while I was still thirty feet away,
and it had nothing to do with my super-cool vampire
powers. Laura was just ridiculously gorgeous, all the
time. So annoying.

Look, it's not envy, okay? Well, not extreme envy.

I'll be the first to admit I'm not one of those pretty girls who pretends she has no idea she's mega-cute. I'm cute; I freely confess. Tall and blonde (big surprise in Minnesota . . . we're about as rare as yellow snow in the dog park), pale skin, light eyes. Never really had to fight the fat, and being undead means I'll be slender forever. The phrase "I'm at my winter weight" no longer has power over me. My senior year I was a contestant in the Miss Burnsville pageant and went home with the Miss Congeniality sash, sort of the "you're not the prettiest or the most talented, but the other gals thought you were nice" consolation prize. I don't exactly drink my water out of a dog dish.

Laura, though.

Breathtaking. Gorgeous. And, as my friend Marc put it, "mouthwatering."

My *gay* friend Marc.

And there she was, standing with someone I didn't know, gesturing wildly in the manner of the native Minnesotan (or, perhaps, *The Omen*). And as I approached, I remembered the *real* reason the Spawn of Satan and My Dead Stepmother made me so uneasy.

Laura was just annoyingly stunning, all the time.

One of those (vomit) natural beauties. Elbow-length hair the color of corn silk. Big blue eyes. First day of spring blue. Cloudless summer day blue. Really, really gorgeous blue. Oh, and thin—did I have to tell you that? I probably didn't have to tell you that.

Great tits, of course, and always primly secured in a 36-B bra. Long legs—she was just a hair shorter than me, and I topped out at six feet—clad in truly faded blue jeans. Not "pre-washed and faded" blue jeans . . . Laura's mom bought them new (yeah, her adoptive mom still bought most of her clothes, though the girl was a student at the U of M). Then Laura wore them and wore them and wore them until they were actually faded, ripped, et cetera. Waste was a sin, after all. Oh! And let's not forget the Spawn of Satan's flawless creamy complexion, courtesy of Noxzema.

And faded running shoes, I realized as I got closer. Also by Target. Running shoes! Who wore those to go buy sandals? She'd have to sit down and pull off her shoes *and* socks each time she . . . Argh, it was going to make me nuts just thinking about it, so I thought about something else. Like the woman she was waving at.

It wasn't a surprise that the Antichrist was talking

to someone; it was a surprise she wasn't followed around by packs of men and women and small children, all the time. In addition to being gorgeous, people just naturally flocked to Laura. Like I said— for the Antichrist, she was pretty nice.

Except, I realized as I got close enough for her to notice me, she wasn't talking to the woman. And she wasn't waving at her, either. Both sets of hands were flying—Laura had either gone deaf, or recently become fluent in American Sign Language.

Oh, and here she is!" Laura's hands, with their long, slender fingers and bluntly short nails, flew as she introduced me. "This is my sister, Betsy. Betsy, this is Sandy Lindstrom." A short, plump woman in her thirties, Sandy brushed her shaggy bangs away from her dark, tip-tilted eyes and smiled at me. "She was wondering when Macy's was having their next sh—"

"November second," I replied automatically. "It starts at eight a.m., an hour before their store usually opens. Park in the West Ramp."

Laura's hands moved in translation—I was always amazed at how cool and mysterious sign language looked—while I jabbered shoe sale tips like a crazed robot.

"Okay, thanks," Sandy Lindstrom mouthed while signing.

"No problem," I said, but she was already turning away, so I started to raise my voice, then realized I was getting ready to shout *"No problem!"* at a deaf person. Instead I turned to my sister. "Who was that?"

"Eh? Sandy Lindstrom."

"Oh. You mean you didn't know her, or—"

"No, but I knew *you'd* be the perfect person to answer her question." Laura grinned and linked her arm through mine. The Antichrist was a toucher and a hugger; did I mention?

"So she was just some random person?"

"Sure." A frown creased Laura's perfect creamy brow. "Why?"

"No reason," I assured her as we began marching past Crabtree & Evelyn, arms linked like half of the cast from *The Wizard of Oz*. The brainless and clueless ("This isn't the Burnsville Mall anymore, Toto") half. "I just didn't know you knew sign language, is all."

"Oh." That short reply was completely unlike Laura; so was the following "shutting up" period that followed. In fact, we were passing Daniel's Leather before she said, "So is this the way to Payless?"

"Payless?" I nearly screamed, coming to such an abrupt stop the Antichrist nearly brained herself on a nearby pillar. "What foul mouth speaks that filth?"

"Mine," the Spawn of Satan replied, straightening up and making sure she hadn't dropped her purse in the near-collision. Laura was a terrific fighter of the undead (weapons of Hellfire, daughter of Satan, et cetera), but not so much a shopper of retail. "You know I'm on a budget, Betsy. We can't all be married to millionaires."

"Undead millionaires," I reminded her, just to see The Flinch—and it came, just as I expected. Which is what a lot of people did at the mention of my husband, Sinclair, King of the Vampires. Hell, half the time *I* still flinched, but usually in irritation instead of fear.

"Yes, well." She fussed a bit, then spotted a mall directory. "Um . . . Payless Shoes . . . 'You Could Pay More, But Why?'" Now it was my turn to flinch at the sound of the dreaded slogan. But why? *But why?* How about because quality costs, you nimrods? How about—"Here it is! One Fifty North Garden."

"Barf Garden." Sure, it was childish. Sue me.

"Oh, come on." She grabbed my arm again—
ugh—and lunged toward the escalator. "You might
see something you like!"

"That's about as likely as you fretting about what
to buy next Mother's Day."

She gasped and wilted, and I had to clutch her
arm to keep her from slithering to the bottom of the
escalator. "Too mean," she reproached, while people headed up the escalator stared down at us with
polite Midwestern curiosity.

"Oh, please. Since when do we pretend she isn't
your mom? Think that's shameful? I admit your
other mom is my stepmom."

"Your dead stepmom."

"Yeah, well, I'm seeing her as often as I ever did."
Disad. #235 about being queen of the vampires: I see
annoying dead people.

"Like I would ever buy her a Mother's Day card
ever."

"Yeah, well, that's why it was a joke, because I'm
not likely to find— Hey!"

Laura had just as abruptly unslithered and
spotted . . . something, because she was now dragging me off the escalator and hauling me toward . . .

a crying child of about three, dressed in typical kid gear of jeans and a MoA T-shirt.

Oh, for— Not again! Laura was always finding/ sensing/communing with lost children. It was one of her superpowers, along with never ever having a pimple.

Look, I have nothing against children. I even have one, sort of. He's my half brother, but also my ward, so I'm his sister/mother. I like kids. But I don't find them like a booger-seeking missile. Laura always does. It's why I won't go to the zoo with her anymore.

Now she was kneeling in front of the dark-haired tyke, chattering away in—um—another language I didn't know. Jeez. Probably shouldn't have dropped out of the U back in the day; they apparently had a fierce foreign languages program.

Ah! Now, predictably, Lost Tyke #16 had forgotten all about crying and was babbling at my sister, who was listening and nodding at every unintelligible word, and would— Ah! The cry of happiness/stress from Lost Mom #16, who had either spotted Laura the Gorgeous and was drawn to her beauty while forgetting about her kid, or had heard her kid's mumbling and zeroed in like—well, like another booger-seeking missile.

Now Lost Mom and Lost Tyke were Reunited Family #16, chattering in response to whatever Laura was chattering; now came the handshakes; now came the sticky but earnest hug from the kid; now came earnest and tearful gratitude from the mother; and now . . . they depart!

"What *is* it with you?" I asked as the Antichrist bounced up to me.

"Only you could make helping a lost child sound like a character defect." She smiled as she said it, so I wouldn't take offense. Laura tried very hard not to offend vampires when she wasn't trying to kill them.

"No, but— And what was that?"

"What?"

"How you were talking to them. What was it?"

"Tagalog." Another curt report, and now she was tugging me toward the hated Payless Shoe Source.

I'd do anything to avoid being immersed in that retail Hellmouth, so I asked, "Tagalong? What's that?"

"*Tagalog.* It's a language."

"Well, I didn't think you three were doing an impromptu play. What language?" Not only did I not know the language, I'd never heard of it, either.

"It's spoken in mmpphhheemes."

Now she wasn't tugging, she was yanking. Curiouser and curiouser. I set my feet, hoping I, intrepid vampire queen, wouldn't actually get into a tug-of-war contest outside Payless Shoe Source with the Antichrist. My reputation! Not to mention my sanity. "I didn't catch that. You want to stop mumbling?"

"It's spoken in the *Philippines*," she almost shouted. "By about twenty-two million people."

"Twenty-two million and one," I joked, and then it hit me. Why the conversation was making her so uncomfortable, when usually only one thing made her uncomfortable. Well, in this case, no wonder. "Wait. You didn't learn Tagalong, did you?"

"Tagalog."

"Or sign language. Oh my God. You didn't learn them; you already knew them. I mean, you just know them. You know them all. Every language . . . you know every language in the world, don't you?"

She shrugged sullenly at me and tried to haul my undead carcass toward the retail Hellmouth, but I wasn't having it. And not just because of the reason you'd think.

"Speak, Laura! You don't mind doing it when strange children are around. Why clam up now? It's part of what you can do, isn't it? You don't like talking about your mom, you don't like other people talking about your mom—and you sure don't like talking about what you *got* from your mom. You just—you know every language. On Earth." Oh, the deals she could haggle in Paris! I was momentarily dizzy at the thought. *Every* language. On Earth. Ever spoken on Earth . . . So she was fluent in Latin and all sorts of other dead languages. Zow! And typical of Laura, she'd never said shit. In any language.

"Just like that movie!"

She was unable to move the bulk that was I, vampire queen. One of my many supernatural abilities. So she quit trying. "What movie?"

"*The Devil's Advocate*. That one where Al Pacino is the devil." The awesomest devil *ever*.

She looked away. If it was possible for someone so gorgeous and nice and smart and occasionally insane to look ashamed, she was. "I never saw it. My parents wouldn't—and then I didn't want—it was about—you know."

Her! It was about her—or her, if she'd been Keanu Reeves in that movie. "So you haven't seen *any*—?"

She shook her head, making her blond waves obscure her face.

"*The Omen*? *The Omen II*? *The Omen III: The Final Conflict*? Or *Rosemary's Baby*? Or *Little Nicky*? Or *Bedazzled*? No, you're not in that one, just your—"

"No, I haven't!"

Except she didn't sound mad. Well, she did, but she also sounded . . . interested?

I peered at her. I knew that look. That was a *my God, those Pradas are on sale!* look if I ever saw one.

"Well, you're gonna," I decided, clamping down on her demonically clammy palm and hauling her—praise Jesus!—away from Payless. "I've got at least half those and we'll Netflix the rest. You're gonna learn all about your heritage—at least, what Hollywood thinks it is. Which, given that they greenlit sequels for *Speed*, *Teen Wolf*, *Legally Blonde*, *Dumb and Dumber*, *Jaws*, and *The Fly*, you should totally take with a ton of salt."

"Have you seen all those?"

"One of my many superpowers," I assured her, hauling her away from the Hellmouth.

**Vampire Queen Betsy Taylor returns in the ninth
novel in the *New York Times* bestselling series from**

MaryJanice Davidson

Undead and Unfinished

Vampire Queen Betsy Taylor is having a tough time
getting through the Book of the Dead—until the
Devil strikes a bargain. She offers Betsy a chance to
finish the cursed (literally!) thing and finally discover
all its mysteries. There's just one catch . . .

Betsy and her half sister, Laura, have to go to Hell
long enough for Laura to embrace her dark heritage
(after a rebellious youth of charity work) and finally
make nice with her mother, aka Lucifer. That means
interacting with their family's past. In doing so,
they're impacting the future in ways they never anticipated. Of course, that's what Mother wanted all
along. Damn her.

penguin.com

M614T1209